# In Case of Emergency

# Also by Keira Andrews

## Contemporary

*Honeymoon for One*
*Beyond the Sea*
*Ends of the Earth*
*Arctic Fire*
*The Chimera Affair*

## Holiday

*Only One Bed*
*Merry Cherry Christmas*
*The Christmas Deal*
*Santa Daddy*
*In Case of Emergency*
*Eight Nights in December*
*If Only in My Dreams*
*Where the Lovelight Gleams*
*Gay Romance Holiday Collection*

## Sports

*Kiss and Cry*
*Reading the Signs*
*Cold War*
*The Next Competitor*
*Love Match*
*Synchronicity* (free read!)

## Gay Amish Romance Series

*A Forbidden Rumspringa*
*A Clean Break*
*A Way Home*
*A Very English Christmas*

**Valor Duology**

*Valor on the Move*

*Test of Valor*

*Complete Valor Duology*

**Lifeguards of Barking Beach**

*Flash Rip*

*Swept Away* (free read!)

# Historical

*Kidnapped by the Pirate*

*Semper Fi*

*The Station*

*Voyageurs* (free read!)

# Paranormal

**Kick at the Darkness**

*Kick at the Darkness*

*Fight the Tide*

*Taste of Midnight* (free read!)

# Fantasy

**Barbarian Duet**

*Wed to the Barbarian*

*The Barbarian's Vow*

# In Case of Emergency

BY KEIRA ANDREWS

*In Case of Emergency*
**Written and published by Keira Andrews**
**Cover by** Dar Albert

**Copyright © 2017 by Keira Andrews**
**Print Edition**

**ISBN:** 978-1-988260-77-8

This is a work of fiction. Names, characters, businesses, places, events and incidents are either the products of the author's imagination or used in a fictitious manner. No persons, living or dead, were harmed by the writing of this book. Any resemblance to any actual persons, living or dead, or actual events is purely coincidental.

# Acknowledgements

Thank you to Leta Blake and Davina Jamison for their invaluable help with this novella.

# Dedication

To everyone who loves the Christmas season as much as I do. May your bells jingle and your winters be wonderlands.

# Chapter One

DANIEL WASN'T SURE how many ways he could say it, but he tried again. "I don't know a Nicholas Smith."

The woman on the other end of the line somehow persisted. "But this is Daniel Diaz?" She rattled off his number.

Daniel took the cell phone from his ear for a moment to glance at the screen. It definitely said Carleton University. Was this some student prank? Did people even make crank calls anymore? He said, "Yes, that's the correct number, but there's been some mistake."

"But you *are* Daniel Diaz, aren't you?"

He sighed. "Yes, but as I said, I don't know a Nicholas Smith." Ugh, he just wanted to get home so he could pack and get back on the road. He was actually taking an honest-to-God *vacation*. With his new, maybe-could-be boyfriend. *Which might be a complete disaster.* Stomach tightening, he pushed away the unease as the woman spoke again.

"I'm so sorry to bother you, but he's one of our students. He's had an accident. Your name and number are listed as his emergency contact."

"I don't know what to tell you. I have no clue who this guy is." He switched his wipers to the next setting, the rubber squeaking a little faster as it cleared the wet snow on the windshield.

Traffic crawled along the slushy 417 toward Kanata, a sea of red lights in the December darkness. Normally Daniel came home after eight and missed rush hour. He usually would've ignored the call while driving, but at five kilometers an hour, he figured he was safe. He really needed to get Bluetooth set up, but most of his communication was by text anyway, even for work. These days the only person who called him was his mother—

"Shit," he muttered with a sinking sensation, gripping the steering wheel, the heated leather warm under his fingers.

"Uh, excuse me?"

"Sorry. It just hit me. Is this *Cole* Smith? Our parents were married for, like, five minutes. It was a million years ago, but a few months back my mom mentioned he was moving to Ottawa. Grad school, or something."

"Yes, Nicholas Smith is enrolled in our master's degree in environmental engineering."

"Why the hell would he put *me* down for his in-case-of-emergency person? We haven't talked in years." He did the math. "*Ten* years."

"Well, I'm not sure. But he's been taken to the hospital, and it's policy that we inform his emergency contact. That would apparently be you, Mr. Diaz."

The woman didn't sound that worried, so it couldn't be a big deal, but... "He's okay, right? It's not anything *serious*?" He barely remembered nerdy, knobby-kneed little Cole, but he didn't want anything bad to happen to the guy.

"All I know is that there was an accident, Nicholas was injured, and an ambulance was called. But, no, I don't believe it's a life or death situation. However, the campus is closing now for the next three weeks, and I imagine Nicholas's classmates are already gone. Yours is the only contact number we have."

*Shit, fuck, fuck.* As the traffic came to a complete standstill, he closed his eyes for a moment and rubbed the bridge of his nose.

"I guess it's up to you whether you go to the ER or not."

Daniel groaned internally. He still had to pack and finish up a couple of hiring reports, even though the office had just closed for the holidays. "God, I hate hospitals."

"Doesn't everyone, Mr. Diaz?"

She had a point, and guilt attacked like a punch to the gut. "Which hospital?"

Of course it was back the way he'd come, and the next exit would take a good ten minutes to reach in the bumper-to-bumper procession. After hanging up, Daniel quickly dialed his mom. She answered on the third ring, and he said, "Hey, Mom. Look, I got a weird call to go to the hospital."

"What? Are you sick?" Her voice squeaked out at a pitch close to something only dogs could hear.

"No, no. I'm fine. Mom? Listen to me. I'm a hundred percent fine. It's about Nicholas Smith. Is that your ex's son?" Not that "ex" narrowed it down. He added, "Cole?"

She sucked in a breath. "Is he hurt? What happened?"

"I don't know yet. I'm on my way. Carleton called me because he had an accident on campus. Do you know why he would have put me down to contact?"

"Because I told him to, darling. He doesn't know anyone else in Ottawa."

"Uh, he doesn't know me either! I haven't seen him in forever." Not since the rebound marriage between Daniel's mother and Cole's father predictably imploded after only six months.

"Of course you know him. He's family. Oh

4

my goodness, what do you suppose happened? Please let him be all right."

"I'm sure he's fine. Don't get worked up." He pushed the heat button on the Audi's dash, turning it down. "And Mom, he is not *family*."

"You don't divorce children, Daniel."

"You got that from *Clueless,* didn't you?"

She huffed. "Regardless, it's accurate."

Daniel wasn't going to argue with her about it. "How's Puerto Vallarta treating you?"

"Divinely! I've already had four mango margaritas and it's not even dinnertime. I wish you could come down, sweetheart. It doesn't seem right spending Christmas without you."

"Mom, you know I'll see you in the new year. Besides, it's a girls' trip with your friends. No men allowed, remember?"

"Yes, true. And at least you're actually taking time off work—although I know you wouldn't if you had your way. Thank goodness Martin believes in work-life balance. You need to learn from your boss, sweetie."

Martin Bukowski, the CEO of AppAny, insisted on being called by his first name, wore flip-flops in Ottawa in January, and had installed a massive tube slide between the floors of his headquarters. The work itself—creating apps for small businesses—was actually rather staid. Lots of back-end web development and whatnot. But Martin was determined his company would be edgy and cool, with playgrounds for offices, flexible work schedules, and a staff with a median age of twenty-five.

"Speaking of work-life balance, Cole is a lovely young man. Assuming he's all right, and pray that he is, maybe you could spend some time with him in the next few months? I'm sure he's been lonely, on his own in a different city."

"I barely have time to see my own friends, let alone some dude I don't even know." He finally reached the off-ramp and circled around to get back on the highway heading into Ottawa. At least there was less traffic going that way.

"As I always point out, you work far too much."

He rolled his eyes. "Yeah, yeah. Mom, I have to hang up now. I can't talk and drive. I'll let you know what's going on with Cole as soon as I can. Love you."

"Love you too, my darling."

He'd heard it a million times that he worked too much, but she didn't understand how important his job was to him. Not many twenty-eight-year-olds made HR director. Granted, he was one of three HR directors working under a VP at AppAny, but it was still an accomplishment.

So what if he worked damn hard? How was that a bad thing? And he was taking a vacation, wasn't he? At the last minute, even!

Daniel thought wistfully of the hot tub waiting. It was outdoor and boasted a view of the mountains and the frozen lake. Mont-Tremblant in Quebec already had a couple feet of snow, and it would be perfect to cuddle up in the steamy water with a glass or three of merlot. Oh, and Justin. Right.

With a mix of excitement and trepidation, he thought of free and spontaneous Justin. He was so handsome, with his strawberry-blond hair, blue eyes, and mouth that didn't quit—in more ways than one. Daniel usually preferred to make plans well in advance, but Justin loved the thrill of doing things on the fly. So Daniel had rented a whole chalet for them last-minute thanks to a cancellation. He could be fun too, damn it.

"It's going to be great," he muttered. "CYC."

It'd been his friend Pam who'd pleaded with him to accompany her to a self-help workshop called CYC: Change Your Cadence. Of course he'd flatly refused at first. He tried to keep Sundays completely free to cook and watch all the mindless TV he'd recorded. Crowding into the Kanata Best Western ballroom with a bunch of unhappy people and paying a hundred bucks to some con artist who promised to change their lives was not appealing in any way, shape, or form.

But tears had glimmered in Pam's eyes as she'd

whispered that no one else would go. She and her wife, Christine—make that ex-wife now—had lived in the condo next to Daniel's rental, where he'd lived for a few years before moving into his new house.

Pam had always been so stoic and practical, the yin to Christine's flighty, over-emotional yang. When it fell apart, Christine took custody of most of their friends in the divorce, and at thirty-three, Pam had found herself starting over.

Daniel had never seen her cry before, so of course he'd gone with her. The guru was an ex-Marine sergeant from the States who'd made a new career for herself after being shot in Afghanistan and then abandoned by her loser husband in the same month. Her philosophy wasn't exactly groundbreaking—if what you've been doing isn't working, try something different—but her delivery captured people's imaginations.

As the other attendees, mostly women but some men, had hopped and twirled and even crawled over the burgundy-and-gray-checked carpet during one of the exercises, literally changing their cadence, Daniel had sat straight-backed in his chair.

Yet Sergeant Becky's message had permeated his consciousness—he still hadn't ruled out brainwashing—and later, after the workshop was over, he found himself often attempting to CYC.

Like with this trip.

He wasn't sure how much he and Justin had in common, but cuddling up together in the hot tub in Mont-Tremblant would be his chance to find out. Before CYC, Daniel would never have agreed to go on a date with someone as…exuberant as Justin, let alone go away with him for a week. And he'd definitely never date anyone in the staff group he managed. Luckily, Justin was under one of the other directors.

Besides, Justin had been so enthusiastic about Daniel, obviously into him and not ashamed to show it. How long had it been since anyone had been interested in that way? It'd been way too long since Daniel have even been willing to attempt a relationship.

*Wonder what Trevor's doing for Christmas.*

Grimacing, Daniel tried to banish the memories, acid flooding his gut. He'd simply been too busy to date the last few years. Okay, *six* years. But he was changing that, wasn't he? CYC. He'd committed himself to doing things differently, so that was that.

He jabbed a button on the steering wheel with his thumb and turned on the radio, an obnoxiously cheery Mariah Carey Christmas song filling the car. He lifted his thumb to change the station, then left it to prove to himself how open-minded he was being.

Justin had pursued him relentlessly at the office over the past month. He worked for AppAny's marketing department as a graphic designer and was fresh out of art school. Justin's attention was flattering, and although Daniel had put him off time and time again, he couldn't deny it was fun to have someone flirting with him. Of course Daniel insisted they keep it strictly professional at the office.

Except for when Justin had blown him in the Audi in the parking lot the previous week.

Usually Daniel could manage his own sexual needs quite handily—so to speak. But it had been an extra-long day and the lot was almost empty. Justin had smiled so prettily and practically begged to go down on him. Daniel hadn't been able to resist. CYC and all that.

They hadn't even actually kissed, but now they'd have a whole week at the chalet to get to know each other. After Daniel dealt with this Cole situation. He took the exit for the hospital, the blue and white neon H on the main building beckoning. What if Cole was really hurt?

"Fuck," he muttered. It was the last thing he wanted to deal with right then, but obviously he had to at least make sure his former stepbrother was okay.

He took a ticket from the machine, the mechanical arm lifting to admit him to the visitor parking lot. The concrete hospital was brightly lit against the dark sky, and Daniel shoved his hands in the pockets of his knee-length Burberry coat. The temperature hovered around the freezing mark, which was balmy for Ottawa in December. He hadn't had to bust out his Canada Goose jacket yet, but he'd bring it to the mountains.

As he walked up to the ER, sirens approached, and by the time he neared the door, he was blinded by red lights and had to jump out of the way as paramedics shouted about a GCS of twelve and a head lac and wheeled in a bloody man on a stretcher.

Daniel followed in the stretcher's wake, stopping in the fluorescent-lit enclosure of the gray waiting room, where a chorus of coughs greeted him. One woman, who was hacking up a lung by the sounds of it, jiggled a wailing baby on her knee. A drunk-sounding man spoke too loudly, evidently to himself, the chairs next to him empty despite the mass of people in the small space, some leaning against walls.

Disinfectant seared Daniel's nostrils, but not enough to cover the stench of—yep, horribly pink vomit being mopped up in the corner. Sad little red and green Christmas decorations hung from the reception desk; one end of the garland trailed onto the floor. A brown-edged poinsettia sat in front of the clerk's computer.

Daniel didn't want to touch *anything*.

A middle-aged woman with a brunette dye job that showed an inch of gray at the roots glanced up as he reluctantly approached the desk. "Can I help you?"

"Yes. I'm here to see Cole Smith? Nicholas, I mean. He was apparently brought in by ambulance this afternoon."

She tapped her keyboard. "You're family?"

To avoid red tape, he nodded and told a big, fat lie. "He's my brother." Working in HR, he knew just how long it could take to deal with privacy regulations.

"He's in curtain seven."

Daniel exhaled. "Does that mean he's okay? Since he's not in the operating room or whatever?"

"Uh-huh. He's just fine." She read from the screen. "Broken hand. Mild concussion. He'll be ready for discharge."

*Thank Christ.* "Thank you so much."

"You're welcome. Go through the double doors to the right."

Another child's wail joined the baby's. Daniel shuddered. "Is it always like this?"

The woman smirked. "Only on a full moon. Fa-la-la-la-la."

Daniel gave her a smile and followed her instructions, pushing through the doors and into the ER itself, where another reception desk sat. The doors shut behind him with a *whoosh*, mercifully dulling the cacophony. A young woman looked up, and Daniel asked, "Curtain seven?"

"Take your first left and look up for the numbers."

In the long, narrow room, machines beeped and someone moaned behind their curtain, but it was mostly still. He felt like he suddenly had to tiptoe, his leather loafers silent on the linoleum anyway. Some curtains were drawn, while others were open, revealing patients on stretchers.

Electrodes dotted the sunken chest of one older man. A silver-haired woman who was likely his wife sat in a plastic chair beside him, gripping his hand. She glanced up as Daniel passed, and he gave her what he hoped was a sympathetic smile. She returned it, then looked back to the man, who snored lightly.

Curtain seven was drawn, and Daniel stood there for a few moments. There was nothing to knock on, so finally he cleared his throat and said, "Uh…Cole? Are you in there?"

# Chapter Two

*H*OLY. *SHIT. DANIEL?!?*

Cole would know that baritone anywhere. It had fueled his teenage fantasies, and even now fire sparked in his veins, his tummy fluttering. Daniel Diaz was a few feet away, only a pale blue curtain separating them. What the hell was he doing at the hospital? How did he know—

Of course. Claudia had messaged Cole on Facebook in the summer when he was registering at school.

*Congrats on the master's program! How exciting! Did you know Daniel's been in Ottawa for some years now? Do you have his number? I'll give it to you. You'll need someone local just in case, but you should call him regardless! I'm sure he'd love to hear from you!*

Cole had been positive it was the last thing Daniel would want considering Daniel had never had time for him when they'd lived in the same house and shared a bathroom. Still, he'd put down Daniel's name and number on the school form as emergency contact—a silly little thing that had made him smile. He'd never expected for a moment said emergency would actually happen.

"Hello? Cole?"

*Shit.* "Uh, yeah?" His voice squeaked on the question, and he cringed, trying to straighten his hair with his right hand, which wasn't enclosed in a cast like his left. He was certain his hair was sticking up at the back of his head, but at least he'd had a trim last week. He sat up a little straighter, the top of the stretcher raised at an angle. "Come in."

The curtain drew back on its rounded track, and *holy shit* there was Daniel. Cole's throat went dry, and he blinked at the vision of hotness before him. He'd seen pics on Claudia's Facebook, but live in person was a whole new level.

Six-one. Dark, shiny curls kept short at the sides and back, a little longer on top. Full lips the color of a blush, and his skin a warm brown—almost golden. He was dressed impeccably, a gray scarf around his throat and a long, black coat that hugged his lean hips.

*Does he have more chest hair now than he did when he was eighteen?*

Daniel frowned. "Cole? It's Daniel Diaz. Do

15

you remember me?"

"Yes!" He winced and lowered his voice. "Sorry. I'm a little out of it. They gave me something for pain. Um, hi. It's great to see you again."

"Yeah. It's been a long time. Look, the school called me. Something about me being your emergency contact."

Cole's gut clenched, and he tasted bile. Shit. Why had he put down Daniel's name? *So stupid!*

Yet Daniel only said, "I was worried, but clearly you're okay. Right?"

"Totally. They insisted on calling the ambulance. Shit, I'm sorry they bothered you." Daniel must have been *pissed.*

His closed-mouth smile was tight. "No, it's fine. As long as you're okay. That's what matters."

Cole blinked. Daniel had pretty much hated him when their parents had been married, but he was being kind of nice now. Granted, it'd been almost a decade. Cole still braced himself, waiting for a sneer. Or worse, to be dismissed altogether.

Nurses passed by with another stretcher, this one holding a drowsy-looking older woman. Daniel stepped closer to let them by, coming in beside Cole now. His eyes were still a hazely-chocolate brown that made Cole think of Ferrero Rocher.

Daniel's dark brows drew together. "Dude, are you sure you're okay? You seem really out of it."

"Oh no, I'm fine!" His head throbbed, but he nodded. "It was stupid. I fell up the stairs. I mean, who falls *up* the stairs? Not even down."

A smile tugged at Daniel's full lips, hinting at the gleam of straight, white teeth. "You always were a klutz, if I recall correctly."

That he remembered *anything* about Cole made him giddy. Cole laughed too loudly. "Yeah. That's me."

Daniel nodded to the cast. "You broke your hand? At least it's not the right one, huh?"

"Yeah! Well, actually, I'm left-handed."

"Oh. Shit." Daniel shifted from foot to foot. "So you don't have any friends here?"

"I made a few at school, but they've gone home for the holidays. And doing a master's isn't like undergrad. A lot of people work part-time. We're all busy, not getting together for keggers every weekend. Everyone already has their own lives." *Except for me.* "You know what I mean?"

"Right. Fair enough."

"Yeah." Cole cringed internally. *Think of something smart to say!*

"No girlfriend, I assume?"

"Why would you assume that?" It was stupid to be offended, but the defensiveness reared up anyway.

Daniel frowned, which seemed to be his default expression, his thick, sculpted brows drawn together. "Because if you had a girlfriend she'd be here?"

"Oh. That makes sense." Now Cole just felt like an idiot. "I haven't had a girlfriend since senior year of high school." He took a deep breath, butterflies flapping in his stomach even though there was nothing to be nervous about. "I came out in university. I'm gay too."

Daniel's eyebrows shot up. "Oh! I didn't realize. Cool. Guess there's no boyfriend either."

"Uh-uh." Cole's cheeks went hot. Daniel must have thought he was so lame. "I was sorry to hear when you and Trevor broke up. Guess that was a while ago now."

Jaw tight, Daniel pulled out his phone, and said in a clipped voice, "Six years. Forever ago."

"Still, I'm—"

"Where's your dad these days, anyway?"

Okay, Trevor was off-limits. Good to know, although he desperately wanted to know what had gone wrong. They'd seemed so perfect together. Cole answered, "He still lives in Toronto in that same house, but right now he's on an African safari with my stepmom."

"Ah." Daniel smirked. "Which number wife is this?"

"Four." Cole shrugged. "It is what it is."

"Yeah, I hear you. My mom's still a serial monogamist too. At least she didn't marry the last few losers. How about your mom? If they were just going to call you Cole, why did they name you Nicholas, anyway?"

"I'm not sure. I'd ask her, but she's dead."

Daniel froze, his eyes going wide. "Shit. I guess I forgot."

"It was six years ago. Car accident."

"Oh. I'm sorry. That really sucks."

"Yeah. Thanks." Cole could think of her now and not cry, which was a vast improvement from the earlier years. Still, he didn't want to dwell, so he asked, "Is your dad still in Spain?"

"Yep. No plans to come back to Canada. He's got a whole new family there, so. You know." Daniel shrugged tightly. "Let me text my mom and tell her you're okay. She was super worried when I told her you were in the hospital."

A rush of warm affection filled Cole. "I'm so sorry to bother her. Claudia's always been wonderful to me. She's stayed in touch. Facebook and stuff." His belly swooped. "Actually, I sent you a friend request when I moved to Ottawa."

"Oh, did you?" Not looking up, Daniel tapped his phone. "I haven't been on Facebook in months. No time."

"Right. I hear you. It's a good way to stay in touch with people from high school and stuff, though."

Daniel glanced up. "Since I have zero desire to

talk to anyone from high school, I'm good."

Right. Likely Trevor-related as well. Daniel and Trevor had been co-captains of the hockey team and out as a couple in senior year, which had blown Cole's little mind at the time. They'd been so *fearless* and had gone off to Western together for university as a total power couple. Cole was dying to know what had gone wrong.

Obviously he didn't ask, instead saying, "I'm sorry to bother you with all this. I'm sure you have much better things to be doing on the Friday before the holidays."

Daniel frowned at his phone as his thumbs flew. "Yeah, I'm driving up to Tremblant to meet my…kind-of boyfriend or whatever. We're staying in a chalet for the week."

"Oh. Sounds amazing." Whoever this "kind-of boyfriend or whatever" was, Cole immediately loathed him simply for existing. Which of course was entirely unfair and immature, but he could accept his shortcomings. "It was really cool of you to come check on me. It's good to see you."

Slipping his phone in his coat pocket, Daniel said, "What? Oh, yeah. Definitely. It's been a long time." His hazelnut gaze ran over Cole. "You're all grown up."

"Still short, but what can you do?" He forced a laugh. *Oh God, shoot me now.*

Before Daniel could reply and prolong their

awkward reunion, the young doctor bustled by and skidded to a halt. "Oh good, someone came after all." She eyed Daniel and said, "I'm Dr. Hanratty. Are you taking Mr. Smith home? Did the nurse go over the concussion protocols with you?"

Cole said, "I'm sure I'll be okay. My head barely hurts. I'll be fine on my own." He sat all the way up, and as if to prove him a liar, the throbbing intensified and a wave of nausea had him salivating.

Dr. Hanratty shook her head, her red ponytail flying. "No, Mr. Smith. You cannot go home alone. I think it's a very mild concussion, but you did bang your head on concrete. Brain bleeds can be sneaky things and can quickly become a life or death matter. You must be observed for twenty-four hours to make sure your symptoms don't worsen. I won't discharge you without someone to care for you."

The idea of being cared for—by Daniel Diaz, no less—sent a pang of yearning echoing through him, but Cole said, "I've already been too much of a pain in the ass. Daniel, don't worry about it. Go to Tremblant. Have an amazing time." Cole had already resigned himself to spending Christmas alone poking at his thesis and marathoning a few Netflix shows. He'd be just fine.

Daniel looked between Cole and Dr. Hanratty, clearly torn. "You don't have anyone else here in

Ottawa who can help?" At Cole's shake of his head, Daniel's shoulders sagged. "It's cool. I'll look after you."

Cole's heart leapt even as he insisted, "Seriously, I'll be—"

"Taken good care of," Dr. Hanratty said in a tone not allowing for argument. "You have a broken hand and a concussion. It's going to be a struggle just to feed yourself. We don't realize how much we use our hands until one is essentially tied behind our backs. Let your friend help."

To Daniel, she added, "You'll need to wake him every two to three hours tonight. Ask him simple questions: his name, the date, who's prime minister. Look for any changes, such as slurring, confusion, increased dizziness. He can take acetaminophen, but no ibuprofen, aspirin, or any NSAIDs. Lots of fluids to stay hydrated, and nothing too heavy to eat for a day or two. He'll likely experience some nausea tonight. He should be just fine, but you need to keep an eye on him. Got it?"

Daniel nodded. "Got it."

"But...he has other things to do!" Over the years, Cole had daydreamed about becoming friends with Daniel. Or maybe more—which was beyond ludicrous, a fantasy he should have outgrown. Still, being a massive burden was not going to make a great first impression. Well, second. Whatever.

Dr. Hanratty gave Cole's leg a pat, ignoring his protestation. "You don't need to stay in bed, but no heavy exercise. Relax and take it easy. No alcohol until your concussion symptoms have cleared. Christmas Eve isn't until when, Wednesday? You should be good to indulge by then."

She leaned down and examined his cast, which was wrapped in alarmingly bright orange medical tape. His thumb was free, but the cast extended from under his elbow to just below his fingertips. "Looks good. Glad the fracture clinic technician was still here. Hours will be cut during the holidays, so they're working late."

Cole grimaced at the orange tape. "And hey, I can pick up extra work waving in planes on the runway."

She laughed. "Ask the nurse for a package of cast protectors for showering. They're shoulder-length gloves vets use to stick their hands inside cows. Take care!" With that, she disappeared around the next curtain.

Daniel was busy frowning at his phone again, and Cole didn't want to interrupt him. Soon after an attendant came with some paperwork, Cole was discharged. At least he didn't have to worry about paying for treatment. Now that he was an adult, he didn't take universal health care for granted anymore.

He cleared his throat. "Um, is everything okay?"

"Hmm?" Daniel glanced up. "Yes. Sorry—had to deal with a work thing. And—hold on." He put the phone to his ear. "Hi, Mom. Yes, like I said, he's totally fine." After a moment, he added, "Just a sec," and passed the phone to Cole.

He took it awkwardly with his right hand. "Hey, Claudia."

"Oh, you poor thing. How are you feeling?"

"I'm fine, really. It's great to hear your voice. The pictures of the resort on Facebook looked amazing. Are you having fun?"

"Having a blast, and it's wonderful to talk to you. Daniel's going to take good care of you."

*Whether he likes it or not.* "He's been great. I'm so grateful. I'd better let you go. Have fun and don't worry about me." He passed the phone back to Daniel, who listened again and uttered a few terse agreements.

When Daniel ended the call, he sighed. "All right. Guess we'd better get out of here. They'll need the bed for someone else judging by the shitshow in the waiting room."

Cole swung his legs around. He was totally fine. Then he stood. "Whoa."

In a blink, Daniel had hold of Cole's shoulders, his hands warm and strong, keeping him steady. "Careful."

Cole tried to smile. "Guess I am a little dizzy."

"Where's your coat? You can't go out in just a T-shirt." Daniel peered around the small area, keeping one hand on Cole as he reached for a plastic hospital bag. He held out the blue hoodie first, and Cole stuck his good arm through the sleeve.

Daniel's fingers brushed the nape of Cole's neck as he pulled the cotton over his left shoulder. A shiver ran down Cole's spine, and he held his breath as Daniel repeated the action with Cole's navy peacoat. He got his hand stuck in the ripped lining before putting his arm in the sleeve.

"Thanks," Cole said, his throat stupidly dry. Up close, Daniel smelled like woody, spicy tobacco, but not in a bad way. In fact, in a way that went straight to Cole's dick. His head swam as he turned, and he wasn't sure if it was the concussion or not.

*Daniel Diaz is actually here. Touching me. I have got to be freaking dreaming.*

Granted, the touch was a solicitous hand on his elbow like one he might give his grandmother, but Cole would take it. As they shuffled past the other curtains, Daniel paused by an elderly couple and asked the woman, "Can I get you anything before I go?"

She smiled, her blue eyes watery. "Oh, thank you, dear. But no, we're all right." She looked at

Cole. "Is this your brother? Glad he's on his way home."

"Oh, he's not—" Daniel stopped abruptly and then said, "Thank you. You're sure you're okay?"

"Yes. Merry Christmas, boys."

They wished her the same before continuing into the hall. Cole asked, "Did you talk to her before or something?"

Daniel shrugged. "No." After a few steps, he said, "We'd better get going. We have to stop by your place and pack a bag."

"And then?" Cole's heart skipped. He'd been so stupidly in love with Daniel. His inner-thirteen-year-old was freaking the hell out.

"Then I guess you're coming on Christmas vacation."

Adrenaline surged through Cole, mixing with painkillers to send his head spinning. *Holy. Shit.* Christmas with Daniel. Maybe being a klutz wasn't so bad after all.

# Chapter Three

PULLING UP IN front of Cole's three-story apartment building, Daniel was lucky enough to find a spot by the curb.

Cole said, "You can just wait in the car. I'll go up and grab my stuff."

Sighing inwardly, Daniel was already unbuckling. "Dude, you're not exactly steady on your feet. Last thing we need is for you to fall and hit your head. Again."

Cole opened his mouth, then snapped it shut. "Good point. I just don't want you to go to any extra trouble."

*Too damn late for that.* Daniel said, "Come on. I have to pack my own stuff. I'd like to get on the road before midnight." It was only just past eight, but still.

Daniel had agreed to look after him, so there was no point in Cole protesting. He reached over and pressed the button to release Cole's seat belt. He'd had to buckle him in too. The doctor was right—apparently they took using both hands for granted.

"Look, I'm sure I really will be fine. I can set the alarm on my phone for every few hours to wake me up."

Daniel raised an eyebrow. "And what? Is Siri going to ask you questions and judge your answers? I don't think the new iOS has a concussion app."

Cole rubbed his face with his good hand. "I just feel like such a dick intruding on your vacation with your boyfriend."

Daniel shifted uncomfortably. "Well, he's not my boyfriend yet." Justin was cute and lively, but would he really make good boyfriend material? Did they have a single thing in common aside from being gay and working at AppAny?

*Chill. The whole point of this trip is to find out. And have some fun for once. CYC.* He checked his phone, finding the lock screen still blank but for the stock image of a random cityscape. He'd texted Justin with the bad news that they'd have company, but no response yet.

"Is he waiting for you to pick him up? I'm sorry to delay everything."

"It's fine—he headed up this aft. And like I told you, there are four bedrooms. It's a big chalet, but it was the only one I could get last minute. Works out for the best. We can do our thing, and you can relax and whatever." *Won't be awkward at all.*

"Right. Okay. Uh... Well, if you're sure?"

He pushed the button to turn off the engine. "I'm sure. It's settled. End of discussion."

"Okay." Cole smiled tentatively. "You were always like that. Once you'd made up your mind, you were determined."

Daniel blinked. "You think so? I'm amazed you even remember me. You were just a little kid."

"Not that young. I was thirteen."

"Were you? I thought you were ten or something. Right, I guess thirteen makes sense since you're in grad school now." Cole had certainly grown up. He was only about five-six, but he had a tight, lean little body, like a swimmer or diver. His short hair was light brown, eyes blue, jaw square, and most importantly, he'd grown into his ears, which had seemed enormous when he was a kid.

Cole seemed okay as they walked into the building and he unlocked the lobby door, but Daniel stayed in arm's reach just in case and asked, "Where's the elevator?"

"There isn't one."

*Of course.* Normally Daniel wouldn't care, but considering stairs had made Cole their bitch once already today... "Tell me you aren't on the third floor."

Cole winced. "I'm not on the third floor?" *Wonderful.*

Progress was steady, though. Cole really was being a trouper, and as he turned the last landing—right hand gripping the railing, Daniel beside him—Daniel said, "You're doing great."

Cole grinned, then stumbled, and Daniel caught him around the waist. "Whoa. Don't get cocky, kid." It wasn't quite a direct quote from *Star Wars*, but as he straightened up, Cole laughed.

"You still love those movies?"

"Sure. It's stupid, I guess." He could still imagine Trevor rolling his eyes at what he'd referred to as "Daniel's little sci-fi problem." He shifted his weight uncomfortably.

Cole blinked at him. "Why would you say that? Those movies are awesome. Did you see the new one when it came out last week? What am I saying, of course you did."

"Actually, I haven't yet," he said with a pang of regret. "Too much work to do before we closed the company for the holidays."

"Seriously?" Cole's thin brows shot up. "I'd have thought you'd be there opening day. I saw it on the weekend. *So* good. You're going to love it." He added, "At least, I think you will. Not that I know you anymore. Or that I ever knew you." His ears went bright red.

"Okay, well. Let's keep going. Carefully." Mindful of the cast, Daniel stood closer, his hand hovering over Cole's back. The stairwell smelled of nothing, really—stale air and concrete, which was better than the stench of piss that made itself home in many stairwells. But now the scent of Cole's sweat and the plaster from the cast filled Daniel's nose.

A strange protectiveness surged up in Daniel as he stayed close to Cole. It sucked being sick or hurt, and it was even worse being alone when you hurt. The previous winter, Daniel had sweat and shivered through a brutal flu, holed up in his room, too weak to even go downstairs for filtered water, refilling his glass at the bathroom sink instead. He'd even missed a day of work.

They reached Cole's apartment without further incident, and since it was approximately the size of a shoe box, it wasn't difficult to stay close to Cole in case of more dizziness. An unfolded futon took up most of the space straight ahead inside the door, and the little kitchen and bathroom stood off to the left.

The place was painted white, and some framed abstract prints that were likely from IKEA decorated two of the walls. A foot-high ceramic Christmas tree sat on a low coffee table, and there were lights taped up above the kitchen cabinets.

Cole said, "I know it's not much, but school's

expensive."

"No, it's…nice. Your dad's not paying your tuition?"

"He did for undergrad. I want to do it all myself now. Really be independent, you know?"

"I hear you." Daniel eyed the only closet. The door stood open, and it held everything from a vacuum to shoes to clothes hanging from an adjustable shower curtain jammed up between the narrow sides. "Do you have a duffel or something?"

Cole did, and of course it was stuffed way in the back of the closet. Daniel pulled his tight slacks up a couple inches for room to move and got on his hands and knees, rooting around until his fingers closed over something that felt like a handle. The duffel bag—blue with the Toronto Maple Leafs logo—was worn but functional. Daniel crawled out and held it up. "Got it."

He'd left Cole leaning against the wall nearby, and Cole nodded and squeaked, "Great." His face was alarmingly red.

"Do you feel sick?" Daniel sprang to his feet.

"Nope! I'm good." He walked slowly toward a battered chest of drawers. A TV sat on top. Opening drawers with his right hand, he awkwardly pulled out a few T-shirts, a hoodie, a pair of jeans, socks, and underwear of the boxer-brief variety.

Daniel scooped the little pile into the bag. Just then, his phone buzzed.

*Hey babe! RU on your way? Np about your bro. The more the merrier! Have surprise 4U, so hurry.*

*We're going to have so much fun!!!*

Cole came out of the bathroom with a Ziploc bag of toiletries and asked, "Is everything okay?"

Realizing he was gritting his teeth at the way Justin used short forms for some words, Daniel unclenched. "Yep. It's all good." So Justin was informal in his texts. Most people were, and just because it drove Daniel crazy didn't make it wrong. He needed to loosen up. That was the whole point of dating Justin. Getting out of his comfort zone. CYC.

Still. Was it really so hard to type out three-letter words?

"I guess we should get going?" Cole asked.

Indeed they should. After the slow and steady trip downstairs, they got back on the road. Daniel lived in a new subdivision in Kanata, and half the streets were still under construction, the dark hulks of half-built houses standing watch. Daniel weaved around potholes made by the construction trucks and equipment.

Cole asked, "Is it noisy with all this being built?"

"I guess. But they don't work weekends, and I leave at six to hit the gym before the office.

They're always done by the time I get home at night. I'm looking forward to all the mess being gone, though." He turned onto his street, strings of Christmas lights adorning some houses. There was also a massive, blinking Santa's sleigh where the little lawn would be in front of the house across the street.

They'd get sod put down in the spring, so currently their front yards were only dirt—now mud covered in wet snow. Daniel pulled into his short driveway and pressed the buttons for the house alarm and then the garage door.

In contrast with his neighbors, Daniel's only holiday decoration was a dark green wreath on the front door decorated with tasteful hints of silver. He'd never put up decorations inside at his condo, and hadn't done it at the house either.

"I'll go in through the garage. Too messy out front. Do you want to just stay in the car? I'll be quick."

"Yeah, cool. The seat warmer is making my butt way too toasty to get out. Do you rent this place?"

"No, I bought it last year. Moved in just before spring."

"Seriously, you have your own house? That's awesome."

Daniel shrugged and said a simple, "Thanks," but he flushed with pride. Only a few feet separated the houses in the cookie-cutter subdivision, but Daniel owned his own fully detached home before he was thirty. While Ottawa was nothing compared to the insane real-estate markets in Toronto or Vancouver, with the rising cost of houses, it was still an accomplishment.

He climbed the three concrete steps up from the garage into the house and unlocked the door. The alarm beeped twice in greeting, and he closed the door behind him and carefully removed his wet loafers. Normally he'd polish them immediately after wearing them in the snow, but they still had a two-hour drive to Mont-Tremblant.

Daniel flipped on the hall light and hung up his coat before hurrying up the stairs, his socks damp on the dark hardwood. He pulled his small suitcase out of the walk-in closet and eyed the racks of clothing, color-coordinated by black, gray, brown, and a few pieces of white. He chose several sweaters and slacks and a pair of dark jeans. Would he need his steamer?

Reluctantly deciding against it, he tugged off his tie and hung it in its place. While the office dress code was insanely casual, he'd always believed in dressing for the job you want. Sure, Martin wore tees or sometimes—Daniel shuddered—Hawaiian shirts, but Daniel always dressed properly. He didn't wear a suit jacket, which was plenty casual enough.

He changed into a charcoal cashmere sweater and a pair of black jeans, then finished packing. Downstairs, he passed through the darkened living room into his open-concept kitchen. The walls in his house were painted a light gray, and all the furnishings and cabinetry were in black and chrome—although he did have a new dark purple rug in front of the black leather couch. CYC.

He opened the fridge and grabbed a couple bottles of water and bananas. Pam always teased him for keeping his bananas in the fridge, but he hated clutter on the gray quartz counters.

After zipping on his shin-high boots, he made two trips out to the vehicle, which was a car/SUV hybrid with a big open trunk space. He tossed his down parka in the backseat since he hated wearing bulky coats in the car. When he slipped behind the wheel, Daniel handed Cole one of the bottles. "There's a holder in your door. Doc said to stay hydrated."

"Right. Thanks. You know you really shouldn't buy bottled water." Still, he uncapped it and chugged half. "It's insanely wasteful. Not just the plastic, but—" He screwed up his face. "Sorry. You don't need a lecture."

"It's okay. You've gone green, huh? I guess as an environmental engineer, you kind of have to. Are you a vegan and all that?"

"God no. I'm way too much of a carnivore.

And I love cheese. Sweet, sweet cheese. So to make up for my evil ways, I lecture unsuspecting people about disposable water bottles. You're welcome."

"Thanks. And hey, I recycle, for the record." Daniel touched the display screen on the dash. "Let me just give Trudy the coordinates."

"Trudy?" Cole chuckled. "You named your GPS?"

Daniel grimaced. "My friend Pam did, and it stuck. I was driving her to Costco and telling her about a woman I had to terminate at our office in Houston." He backed out of the driveway, ignoring Trudy's redundant directions for leaving the subdivision. "So I called her into the term meeting—"

"Wait, is that the euphemism for firing someone?"

"Yes. Anyway, most people cry and sometimes try to bargain, or there's denial. Definitely lots of shock, understandably. But once in a blue moon, we'll get a runner. Trudy stormed out and was cursing at the top of her lungs in the workspace. I went after her, hissing, "Trudy! Trudy!" I was afraid I'd have to call security to tackle her, but she calmed down. Anyway, I was telling Pam the story, and the GPS kept interrupting, so Pam declared it was Trudy's revenge."

Cole laughed. After a few moments, he asked, "Does it bother you? Firing people?"

A curl of dread wove through him, but Daniel shrugged as he turned onto the main road. "I don't enjoy it, but it has to be done sometimes. If profit margins go down, the company has to reduce spend and HC." He always felt sick to his stomach before a firing, but he had to do his job.

"HC?"

"Sorry. Head count. Also, if we acquire another company, we look for synergy opportunities. Weed out duplicated roles and try to consolidate business functions. Usually layoffs really have nothing to do with the staff members themselves. Which doesn't make it easier to take, I realize."

Daniel had often suggested that they could cut costs by not hiring executives who earn a quarter million a year for their ideas and didn't actually do the operational work, but for all of Martin's insistence on innovation, prestige still mattered. Daniel was the one who had to do the firing, so Martin got what Martin wanted.

"Do you have to do it often?"

"Several times a year, I guess. They send me to our other offices too. The one in Houston, and another in England. I don't get emotional, so I'm effective."

Pam's teasing voice echoed in his head: *It's because you're cold and dead inside. You really need to work on that.*

"Mmm."

Cole sounded sleepy, and Daniel glanced over after he checked his blind spot and accelerated onto the highway. They were heading back past Ottawa, then across the Ontario/Quebec border toward the Laurentian Mountains. Daniel said, "Go ahead and sleep."

"Sorry. I'm super tired all of a sudden." Cole leaned his head back, eyes drifting shut. He murmured, "Cars always put me to sleep. My mom said when I was a baby she used to drive me around the block and I'd be out like a light."

"Plus you have a concussion. Sleep. I'll wake you up in a little while to check on you."

Daniel put the satellite radio on low, the murmur of commercial-free Christmas carols keeping him company, along with the steady rhythm of Cole's deep breathing. It was strangely comforting that Cole trusted him enough to fall asleep while Daniel was driving. They hadn't seen each other in ten years, yet here they were. Life could be incredibly bizarre.

Flurries fell, a blanket of white over the fields, the temperature fortunately dropping. Daniel far preferred the frigid, snappy cold to the slushy mess around the freezing mark. The roads had been salted and were only a little icy, and there weren't many cars around. As Sarah McLachlan sang a melancholy yet pretty song about a river, the world seemed hushed and peaceful.

An hour and a half passed before Cole whimpered and moaned, lifting his head. "Fuck me. I think I'm going to be sick."

Daniel checked his blind spot and veered onto the empty shoulder. The amount of detailing needed to scrub vomit out of his interior was not something he wanted to deal with. He unbuckled Cole's seat belt before hopping out and running around to help him climb down, shivering in the cold, their breath pluming icily.

Cole took a few steps before bending in half and blowing chunks into the fresh snow. *Ugh.* Clearly Dr. Hanratty was correct about the nausea. Cole leaned his good hand on his knee, spitting and groaning. He seemed stable enough, so Daniel leaned back into the car to flip on the hazards and grab a box of mints from the glove compartment. He uncapped Cole's water bottle, handing it over as Cole straightened up with another groan.

"I haven't puked on the side of the road since high school."

"You partied in high school? Huh." Daniel rubbed his hands together and blew into them, stepping from side to side to keep moving in the cold. He brushed snowflakes off his sweater.

Cole swigged some water, sloshing it around his mouth before spitting it back out. "Nerds skimmed off the top of their parents' liquor bottles too."

"Ah, swamp water. I don't miss those days. Here, have a mint or five." He pulled the tin from his pocket and opened it.

"Thanks." Cole popped a few mints into his mouth and glanced around, moving his head gingerly. "Think it's okay to piss out here?"

The Audi's headlights cut through the night, but otherwise it was all dark. "Go for it."

Daniel stayed within arm's reach as Cole bent his head to unzip. Cole fiddled with his fly, cursing under his breath. "Fuck. I can't get the button."

"Oh. Um…" *Shit.* Well, he'd agreed to play nurse or whatever, so… "Here." Daniel stood in front of him, hoping the puking had definitely stopped. He couldn't see what he was doing, so he stooped and undid the button on feel and pulled down the zipper. He stood straight. "There."

Cole's sharp puffs of sour-yet-minty breath hit Daniel's throat where his sweater made a small V. "Thanks." Cole's voice was hoarse, probably from the cold night air. Not to mention the puking.

"Are you good now?"

"Uh…" Cole was tugging his underwear with his right hand, and he huffed, "Jesus, why couldn't I be ambidextrous?"

Daniel laughed awkwardly. *This isn't super weird or anything.* "Here, I'll just…" He pulled down Cole's underwear a few inches, his knuckles brushing wiry hair. Nerdy little Cole was definitely

41

a man now. Cole's belly was taut and trembling, and more puffs of his quick exhalations warmed Daniel's skin.

Cole's laugh sounded strained. "I can pull my dick out. I hope." His fingers brushed Daniel's, and Daniel whipped his hands back. After a few moments, Cole said, "Are you into golden showers?"

"*Huh*? Oh, right!" He sidestepped out of the way. "Fire at will."

As Cole pissed into the snow, Daniel looked away, crossing his arms, debating whether to grab his coat from the back. Cole had to be freezing too in his hoodie. But soon enough, Cole said, "Can you just get the button? I managed the rest."

Daniel jolted at the sound of Cole's low voice. "Sure." He did it up, his numb fingers fumbling a bit, then he helped Cole back up into the passenger seat. Once he was settled, Daniel leaned across him to hook in the seatbelt.

Cole was motionless, and Daniel said, "You can breathe. I won't bite."

"No, I know." He laughed, clearly uneasy. "Thanks for your help. I'm sorry for the grossness and having to stop."

"Don't worry about it. We're almost there anyway."

When he was back in the car, Daniel flipped the seat and steering wheel heaters back on and swiped again at the snowflakes melting on his sleeves.

Cole said, "You've got some in your…" He lifted his left arm as if he was going to brush the snow away from Daniel's hair himself, then sucked in a breath. "Fuck. That hurts. Right. Broken hand."

Daniel brushed a palm over his head. "I'd think it would be hard to forget."

Cole wiped the snow from his own hair. "You'd think." He sighed. "Dude, I'm sorry you got stuck with me. You weren't planning on having a third wheel on your romantic vacay."

He bit back a surge of irritation. Beating a dead horse wouldn't change anything. "I wasn't, but shit happens. It is what it is. I made up my mind, remember?"

"I'm still grateful. This was a big ask considering we haven't even seen each other in ten years."

It was, but Daniel couldn't exactly leave Cole helpless. "For once and for all, don't worry about it. Besides, you know my mom is thrilled that we're 'reconnecting' as she'd say."

Cole smiled. "True. And…" He turned his head to look out the window. "I think it's cool too. Reconnecting."

Daniel didn't know what to say, so he went with, "Yeah," and turned up Kelly Clarkson singing very enthusiastically about a Christmas tree.

After another thirty kilometers, the warm glow of the village came into sight nestled at the bottom of the mountains soaring above. Cole sucked in a breath just as Trudy instructed Daniel to turn off the main road.

Cole said, "Wow. It looks like a postcard."

It really did. There was a cluster of colorful, mostly three-story buildings sandwiched together like gingerbread with fresh snow covering the roofs, a clock tower jutting up at one end of the village, and golden Christmas lights everywhere. Daniel had never really been one for the holidays, but it was gorgeous and welcoming.

Trudy directed them around the village and eventually onto a road that was surely dirt under the snow. It was a little icy, and he navigated the turns slowly.

"You have arrived at your destination."

The lights of the chalet glowed around the bend of a short driveway, and Daniel followed Justin's tire tracks, which were half-covered in the fresh snow. A minivan sat outside the chalet, and he pulled up beside it and turned off the car.

"Whoa," Cole breathed. "This place is gorgeous. All those windows!"

The two-story chalet had massive windows on both floors, and the listing had promised no neighbors for two kilometers on either side. Away from the lights of the village, it was too dark and cloudy to make out the view of the lake and mountains, but Daniel buzzed with excitement at the thought of seeing them in the morning. It really had been too long since he'd taken a vacation.

"It looks so peaceful," Cole added.

"It does." The owner had strung multicolored Christmas lights around the rail of the wraparound porch, and the effect was magical. Daniel opened the car door and stopped with one foot hanging out, baffled.

What was that thumping? A moment later he realized it was music. A tendril of unease unfurled. Huh. Well, perhaps Justin found techno relaxing? Daniel hoped it wasn't carrying over the frozen lake and disturbing anyone.

He grabbed his parka and put it on, leaving it unzipped as he walked around the car. Cole had managed to unbuckle himself and was standing there waiting with a frown, trying to shrug his good arm into his coat. Laughter and voices echoed. Voices.

Plural.

As Daniel's heart pounded in time with the bass, Cole said, "Uh, I didn't realize you were having a bunch of people up for a party?" His breath came out in frosty plumes in the frigid air.

"I'm not," Daniel managed to grit out, his jaw clenched. "Justin said he had a surprise, but…"

But surely he knew better than this.

After helping Cole with his coat, Daniel marched up the walkway, which had likely been cleared that morning and was now covered by an inch of fresh snow. The wraparound porch had been cleared earlier as well, and he walked around the corner of the chalet toward where the hot tub sat in a sort of sunroom with glass doors that could be folded back, leaving it open to the elements but for the wooden roof.

Full beer bottles were wedged into the snow, empties discarded on their sides on the porch. Smoke drifted on the breeze—marijuana and cigarette. It was an eight-person hot tub—nice and roomy for two. Currently it held six goddamned people, including Justin, who realized with a joyful shriek that Daniel was standing there.

"Dan! Finally! Get your clothes off and get in here!" He stood, displaying his red Speedos, which hugged his package and showed off his muscled body.

The other occupants of the hot tub turned and waved, and Dan recognized them all from the office. A web writer named Melody—no, Melanie—squealed, "Hi, Dan!"

Justin spread his toned arms. "Surprise!"

As anger and awful, sticky humiliation spread through him, Daniel could agree it sure as hell was.

# Chapter Four

*A*WWWKWARD.

Tension radiated so powerfully off Daniel that Cole was amazed the heat of his fury didn't melt the snow in a radius around him. Everyone in the hot tub looked to be in their twenties and in various states of wastedness.

The porch rumbled with the bass of the music coming from inside, the massive windows actually rattling. Cole's head pounded mercilessly. He just wanted to go to bed, but clearly that had to wait.

A redheaded guy glared at the Speedo-wearer, who was presumably this Justin, Daniel's maybe-boyfriend or whatever. In a Quebecois accent, the redhead demanded, "Justin, what do you mean, surprise?" To Daniel, he called, "You didn't know we were coming for the weekend?"

The Asian girl in pigtails who had greeted Daniel excitedly now exchanged worried looks with the blond guy she was cuddled up with. She shouted to Justin, "Did you seriously not tell Dan we were coming?"

"It wouldn't be a surprise if I did!" Justin splashed out of the hot tub, grabbing a terrycloth robe and shoving his feet in flip-flops, hopping around. "Brrr, it's freezing!"

*No shit, Sherlock.* Justin was blond and lean and had six-pack abs. He was objectively handsome, but *ugh.* He was clearly a douche and a half. Cole found it hard to believe Daniel was dating him.

As Justin approached Daniel, he batted his eyes. "Come on, Mr. Grumpy. Warm me up. You'll have fun, I promise." He reached out.

Thank the *lord*, Daniel held him back with a firm hand on Justin's chest. "I don't think so. Turn that music off. It's way too loud."

Justin rolled his eyes. "Oh, come on. Take that stick out of your ass already. We're on vacation! Let's party!"

Daniel's nostrils flared, and Cole thought he might be about to witness a homicide. Completely justifiable homicide. Pushing past Justin to the sliding glass door, Daniel disappeared inside.

Again, Justin rolled his eyes and asked Cole, "Has he always been so uptight?"

Before Cole could tell him to go fuck himself, the music was silenced. In the sudden quiet, the hot tub bubbled, its motor a low hum. Fat snowflakes drifted down, the Christmas lights wrapped around the porch railing casting a warm, colorful glow. The forest and lake beyond seemed utterly still.

A brunette with long, damp curls and a halter bikini top belched, then laughed uproariously, along with Justin and another hairy dude. When the laughter died down, she said, "Justin, get me another beer."

Cole left them to it, following into the house. Daniel had left his boots by the door, and Cole did too, closing the sliding door behind him. The chalet was gorgeous—a vaulted ceiling, exposed beams, light pine wood everywhere. An interior stone accent wall contained a fireplace, where logs smoldered. Two of the exterior walls were largely glass. The kitchen was down a short corridor to the left, just after a staircase that presumably led up to bedrooms in the rear of the house.

Red, green, and gold Christmas decorations sat on shelves, garlands and lights wrapping the railing on the staircase. Two gold stockings even hung from the mantle over the fireplace. There was a fresh pine tree filling the corner past the fireplace. The tree was bare, but boxes surrounded it. Decorations, presumably.

Had Justin arranged all that? Cole glanced back through the glass at where Justin was taking a hit off a joint, apparently utterly unconcerned that Daniel was furious with him. Nope. Seemed highly unlikely Justin had done anything thoughtful.

On socked feet, Cole approached Daniel, who stood at the foot of the stairs, still wearing his parka. From behind, Cole couldn't see his expression, the hood of his coat blocking his profile as well. He was stock still, fists clenched.

It seemed stupid to ask if he was okay. Instead, Cole said, "You used to hate being called Dan." Also stupid, but he had to say something.

The sliding door opened behind Cole, admitting the three people who hadn't seemed happy with Justin's surprise. As they approached, wrapped in towels, Daniel said, "I still do. I hate being called Dan."

The Asian girl stopped short. "Shit, seriously? But everyone at work calls you Dan."

Daniel turned and shrugged tightly. "Martin calls me that, so after a while I stopped trying to fight it."

"Oh." She smiled nervously at Cole. "Hi. You're Dan's—Daniel's brother? I'm Melanie." She motioned to the blond guy, who had slipped an arm around her wet shoulders. "This is my boyfriend Paul, and that's Jean-Luc."

The redhead nodded. "Bonjour."

"Hey. I'm not really Daniel's brother."

Melanie blinked. "Sorry. I thought Justin said…"

"We were stepbrothers ten years ago," Daniel said. "Not for very long. Anyway, to answer your question out there, no. I had no idea anyone would be here but Justin."

Paul groaned. "I had a bad feeling about this. Didn't I say that, Mel?"

"You did, babe." Through the glass, the other girl shrieked in the hot tub, and Melanie huffed. "Fucking Louise. She and Mike are idiots, but I figured they'd be fun to party with. Of course I also thought we were invited. Justin said you were totally cool with us coming up just for the weekend, and then you'd have your romantic vacation after."

Daniel practically vibrated. "Safe to say the romance is off."

"We will leave in the morning," Jean-Luc said. "And take Justin with us, yes?"

"Definitely." Daniel shrugged out of his coat and marched to the closet tucked into an alcove before the passage to the kitchen.

Cole winced as he struggled out of his. Melanie said, "Do you need help? God, the last thing you needed was more drama, huh? How are you feeling? What happened?" She peeled Cole's coat off his shoulders.

"I'm fine. Thanks. I tripped and fell. I'm a

massive loser."

"You are not," Daniel snapped. He exhaled and softened. "I'll get you some more water." He disappeared into the kitchen.

Melanie whispered to Cole, "We'll just leave you guys to it."

Paul asked, "Are the keys still in the car? I'll get your bags."

"I think so? It's a keyless car, but all Daniel's stuff is in there, so it should be unlocked if the keys are in his bag."

Cole gave them an awkward little wave and followed into the kitchen, grateful that not everyone who'd crashed was an asshole. Daniel stood by the fridge, as if he was going to open it and forgot what he was doing. He muttered, "I'm such an idiot. CYC my ass."

"See…what?"

Daniel rubbed his face. "It's too moronic to even repeat."

Cole hated seeing Daniel beating himself up. "Maybe it'll help to talk about it. It might stop you from drowning your boyfriend in a hot tub."

"Oh, he is *so* not my boyfriend and never will be. Which I *knew*, but I kept telling myself to get out of my comfort zone and try new things."

"I have to admit he doesn't quite seem like your type. Unless your type has become dickbags."

Daniel laughed harshly. "One could argue it

always was."

Man, what had gone so wrong with Trevor? Clearly now was not the time to ask, so Cole said, "It's not your fault."

"Of course it is!" Daniel spun to face him, opening his mouth to say more and stopping short. "Are you okay?"

Cole realized he was grimacing, the throb in his broken hand growing stronger, along with his headache. "Yeah. It just hurts."

"You need to rest. I know what to do, but I'll find a concussion checklist just in case." He pulled his phone from his pocket. "Crap, I need the wifi password. No service out here."

A young woman wearing a bikini with an open parka over it clomped into the kitchen. This was Louise, apparently. "The wifi works for shit. We're basically incommunicado out here."

Daniel barked, "Boots off in the house!"

Opening the fridge, she jumped, then looked down at her feet and back to Daniel. "It's not like it's your house. What do you care?"

"First off, it's rude to drip all over someone else's hardwood. Second, I'm the one paying for any damage, aren't I? Boots. Off. In. The. House."

"Okay, geez." Louise took a case of beer off the bottom shelf, heaving it up with a grunt and disappearing back outside.

"Fuck," Daniel muttered. There was a thick

binder on the island that said *Welcome!* He flipped it open, presumably scanning it for the password. He tapped the screen and waited. And waited. "Shit. I can't check my work email if the wifi isn't connecting."

Cole refrained from reminding him he was supposed to be on vacation now, since, to be fair, as vacations went this one sucked so far. Instead he asked, "Um, where should I sleep?"

Daniel rubbed his face. "You can take the master bedroom. I'll sleep on the couch or something."

Flip-flops slapping wetly, Justin appeared and gave Daniel a heavy-lidded look and sly smile. "Come on now, Grumpy. I thought *we* were taking the master."

"I thought we'd be here alone," Daniel snapped. "I thought a lot of things. Just in case it's not clear, whatever this was between us? Is done."

Eyes red from the pot, Justin rolled his tongue in his cheek and treated them to a textbook expression of bitchface. "Fine. I'll bunk in with Louise. You and your little brother can take the master." He turned on his heel and stalked off. *Slap-slap-slap.*

Cole couldn't believe the nerve of the asshole, but kept quiet. "If there's a king bed, I'm sure it'll be fine," he said, and not just because sharing a bed with Daniel was a wet dream come true after a decade.

"Right." Daniel exhaled forcefully. "Let's grab our stuff and check it out."

There was definitely a king bed—a mammoth that was almost as wide as Cole's living room. The duvet was a tasteful navy blue with faint pinstripes, the room decorated in brown and green accents. The same light pine hardwood seemed to run through the entire chalet.

Daniel took Cole's duffel off his shoulder and placed it by the long dresser with his suitcase. Then he gathered up Justin's things and threw them into the hallway.

Cole slipped into the bathroom, which was so big he almost had to go around a corner to spot the toilet beyond a shower stall and soaker tub. The long double vanity closest to the door was made of smooth granite. The tiles on the floor and shower were white and gray with navy accents, and every surface gleamed.

Bending over the near sink, Cole managed to splash water on his face with his right hand. When he stood straight, Daniel was there behind him, waiting with a towel. Heart thumping, Cole gave him a little smile. "Thanks." He dried his face. "I just want to brush my teeth and go to sleep."

"I'll get your stuff," Daniel said, returning shortly with Cole's battered and soap-stained toiletry bag. "Here, let me help you…"

Turning and leaning his butt against the counter, Cole lifted his good arm, concentrating on breathing evenly as Daniel stood close and peeled off his hoodie and tee, then undid his jeans. They pooled at Cole's feet, and he kicked them free before Daniel could kneel. Because if Daniel kneeled in front of him, Cole would spontaneously come in his underwear.

While Daniel went to grab Cole's PJs, Cole reached down with his right hand and stripped off his socks. Daniel returned with the plaid red and blue flannel and said, "Easier if you go shirtless, right?"

"Uh-huh." Cole's nipples were tight peaks even though the bathroom was warm, the floors heated beneath his bare feet. He stepped into the plaid flannel pajama bottoms, holding his breath as Daniel tied the drawstrings into a loose bow. "Thanks."

Cole turned back to the sink, unsurprised to glimpse in the mirror that his blush crept all the way down to his sternum. He managed to unzip his bag, but after a few attempts at uncapping the toothpaste with the tube wedged against his hip for leverage, he gratefully handed it to Daniel, who'd been waiting and watching.

Cole tried to laugh. "I really am helpless."

"Anyone would be. I'm sure you'll get the hang of stuff in the next few days." Daniel took out Cole's toothbrush and turned on the cold water to wet it before neatly squeezing a line of paste onto the bristles.

*The next few days.*

Pulse skittering, Cole shoved the toothbrush in his mouth, trying to hide a burst of giddiness that temporarily eclipsed the pain. In the morning, Justin and the others would leave, and it would be Cole and Daniel alone for a whole week.

*A whole week when absolutely nothing romantic will happen, so slow your roll.*

Cole rinsed, spitting into the sink and talking himself out of getting carried away. Surely nothing would ever happen between them, but still. Just being friends would be amazing.

While Daniel disappeared back into the bedroom, Cole managed to tug down his PJs and undies enough to piss on his own. *Victory!* He left the bathroom light on for Daniel, stopping short as he reentered the bedroom. Naked, Daniel faced the other direction as he bent over and stepped into black pajama bottoms that looked like they might be silk.

Thighs and buttocks flexing, he straightened, pulling up the pajamas, which sat low on his lean hips. A lamp on the bedside table sent warm light over Daniel's golden-brown skin, and Cole swallowed thickly, his throat gone dry.

As Daniel pulled on a white tee and turned,

Cole hurried around to the far side of the bed closest to the door. He pulled back the duvet and carefully climbed in, praying his twitching dick would at least stay soft until he was hidden. It was so inappropriate to want him this badly when Daniel was only being kind, but he couldn't stop the desire heating his blood.

Daniel walked around the bed and put a tall glass of water on the side table. "Drink some of this. You'll note it's not in a plastic bottle."

Cole smiled. "Thanks."

"I'll wake you up in two hours and make sure you're okay."

He drank, then gingerly lay down and got settled on his back, trying to find just the right position so his hand didn't ache too much. The mattress was so wide he barely felt the dip when Daniel got under the covers and switched off the lamp. There was about a foot gap between the dark curtains, casting just a little bit of light from outside.

The odd whoop and burst of laughter and chatter echoed up from the hot tub, but it was distant, the walls of the chalet clearly solidly built. From what Cole could glimpse through the window, it was still snowing and the moon had peeked through as midnight neared.

So. Here he was. In bed with Daniel Diaz. No big.

Amid the physical pain, his heart raced, skin tingling. He peeked at Daniel from the corner of his eye. Daniel was on his back too, staring at the ceiling. There were so many questions Cole wanted to ask, but now that he was in a big, fluffy bed—the mattress one of the awesome soft kinds like at hotels—he couldn't resist the undertow of sleep, his eyes closing as he gave up the fight.

"COLE. WAKE UP."

"Mmm." Cole groaned. He ached, and he just wanted to sleep. Why was there light? Who was he dreaming about? That deep voice was so familiar…

"Cole. Open your eyes."

He groaned. That voice sent a tingle to his balls. Almost sounded like Daniel. Where was that light coming from? Groaning again, he forced his eyes open, blinking up at someone who looked exactly like Daniel and—oh! It all flooded back with a jolt of adrenaline. They were sharing a bed at the chalet, and currently Daniel was right beside Cole on the mattress, leaning over him.

"What's your name?" he asked.

"Cole Smith. You're Daniel Diaz."

A smile tugged on Daniel's lips. "Yes, I am. I'm supposed to ask the questions before you answer. Where do you go to school?"

"Carleton, but my program is a joint thing with U of O. Can I have more water?"

Daniel leaned over him to get the glass, then helped Cole lift his head to sip. It was nuts to think that less than twenty-four hours ago, Cole had woken alone in his tiny apartment, ready for another day of research in the library.

Aunt Judy had invited him to spend the holidays with her family, but he hadn't wanted to blow his money on the flight to Winnipeg. So he'd opted to spend Christmas alone with his books and Netflix, and it was just *fine*.

But Cole had to admit it was a hell of a lot better waking up to his teenage fantasy in bed with him. He took another swig and shook his head when Daniel offered more water.

Daniel asked, "What are you studying?"

"Environmental Engineering. Specializing in water and wastewater treatment."

"Huh. That sounds really cool. You'll have to tell me about it when you're not concussed. How do you feel? Any dizziness or new symptoms?"

"I don't think so. Can I go back to sleep now?"

"Yep." Daniel rolled away and switched off the lamp, plunging the room into darkness.

"Wake up, Cole."

This time, Cole remembered where he was and why Daniel was there, a squiggly burst of excitement fluttering in his belly. He hurt, but it was wonderful to know he was safe and protected before he even opened his eyes.

*Daniel's here. I'm okay.*

Maybe it was crazy to feel that way when it had been ten years since he'd seen the guy, but he trusted Daniel. He wished he could burrow close and feel Daniel's arms around him.

That wasn't in the cards, so he pried his eyes open, blinking in the lamp's glare. Daniel helped him take two Tylenol and finish the glass of water, then drilled him on the basic facts of his life.

After, Daniel nodded and flicked off the light. "I'll set the alarm for three hours this time."

Exhaustion tugged dully at Cole along with the thudding pain, but he felt strangely awake. As his eyes became accustomed to the dark, he watched snow hit the narrow strip of visible window pane. Before he could talk himself out of it, he asked, "What did you mean before? About 'see why' something?"

In the hush, he wasn't sure Daniel would answer. Then Daniel replied, "Go back to sleep."

"I can't. Talk to me for a bit?"

Again, silence. Then after a few heartbeats, a sigh. Daniel rolled onto his back from where he'd been curled facing the window. He murmured,

"It's an acronym. CYC. Change your cadence. I went to a stupid self-help seminar with my friend Pam. This ex-Marine wrote a book on it. Change your cadence—you know, change it up, do things differently. I figured I had nothing to lose by trying." He laughed scornfully. "Nothing but my dignity."

"Justin's the one with no dignity. You rented this amazing place for him and he takes advantage of that? Screw him."

Daniel was silent a few moments. "I just feel so stupid. I ignored all my instincts. Because of a *self-help* seminar."

"It could be worse. You could have joined a cult." Daniel's chuckle warmed him. *I made him laugh!* Cole added, "You could be wearing a toga right now or be preparing for the coming of our alien overlords."

Daniel laughed again. "I guess that's true."

"I've been told they'll be merciful. Mark me down as dubious, but willing to be convinced if the aliens look like Han Solo." He pondered it. "I guess all the humans in *Star Wars* are actually aliens, aren't they?"

"Of course. Anyone not from Earth is technically an alien. And I'm with you. Hot Han Solo aliens can stay." He was quiet for a few long moments. "Thanks, Cole. You grew up pretty cool."

*I'm cool! Daniel Diaz thinks I'M COOL!*

Cole cleared his throat. He wasn't thirteen anymore. He needed to rein it in. "Yeah. You too." He shifted to stretch the crick in his neck, wincing as pain shot up his arm, then back down again like a pinball machine of *ouch*.

Daniel was suddenly close, saying, "Are you okay?" In the darkness, Cole could just make out the gleam of his eyes and the concern clear in them. His belly flip-flopped. *He's only being nice. Don't read anything into it.*

Cole managed to smile. "I keep forgetting about my hand. Not sure how, since my whole arm throbs. On the bright side, I think my head hurts a little less. Or it's numb. Whichever."

"Right. Cool." Daniel scooted back to his side, and Cole told himself he was imagining that he was cold now. Still, he tugged up the duvet with his good hand.

Daniel said, "We should sleep."

"Mmm." Cole had so many more questions to ask, but his eyes were heavy, and he knew Daniel would be there in the morning.

# Chapter Five

THE WEIRDEST THING about waking up in bed with his former stepbrother was how it didn't actually feel that weird.

Through the gap in the blackout curtains, pale light flowed into the room. On his side with his back to the windows, Daniel could make out Cole's slack face a couple of feet away on the huge bed. Cole had tried to roll onto his side a few times, hissing in pain before resettling on his back and falling asleep again. His head faced Daniel, and every so often he whimpered in his sleep.

The duvet had slipped down to his waist, but it was warm in the room. Cole's chest was smooth and surprisingly toned. His nipples were pinkish more than reddish—not that it mattered. Daniel didn't even know why he was thinking about it. He shook his head and reached over to gently tug up the duvet.

It was definitely surreal to be there with Cole. But not unpleasant. Daniel hadn't shared a bed with anyone since Trevor, platonically or otherwise. Cole was virtually a stranger, yet there was a level of comfort between them that must have been a product of living together years before.

He didn't remember much about Cole from the short period their parents were married. Daniel had known it wouldn't last, and he'd been eager to finish high school and get away. He didn't recall thinking much about Cole one way or the other.

But adult Cole was a good listener, and being holed up with him was a refuge from Justin's assholery. Something about whispering in the dark during the night had dislodged a memory that kept playing through Daniel's head now.

The bathroom he and Cole had shared was sandwiched between their rooms with a door on each end. They'd kept the doors ajar, usually closing them when the bathroom was in use.

*He got up to piss in the night, not needing to turn on the light as he padded to the toilet, and not bothering to close the doors. When he finished and tucked himself back into his boxers, a little voice called out.*

*"Daniel?"*

*He went to Cole's door and stuck his head through the gap. "Uh, yeah? You sick or something?"*

*In his twin bed under the Leafs posters plastering*

*the walls, Cole sat up. "No. I just wanted to say I think you and Trevor are awesome. You're so brave."*

*Daniel blinked. "Oh." Shame burned his cheeks. He'd pretty much ignored the kid since their parents got together. "Um, thanks." He tried to think of something else to say, and went with, "You should go back to sleep."*

It had been the night after Daniel had brought Trevor home for dinner and they'd announced they were gay and in love. Daniel could admit now that, deep down, he'd been hoping his mom and Cole's dad would freak out. It hadn't been about bravery at all, but a petulant desire to cause trouble.

*Ugh. I was such an asshole.*

His phone buzzed, and he reached over to touch Cole's good shoulder, barely grazing his skin. "Cole. Wake up." Cole murmured, and Daniel wriggled closer, reaching across to wrap his hand fully around Cole's shoulder. "Hey." He squeezed.

Cole opened his eyes with a start, tensing. "Huh?"

"Shh. It's okay." Daniel squeezed gently again, Cole's shoulder warm beneath his palm. "Time for your quiz. What's your name?"

He relaxed, yawning widely. "Cole Smith."

"Who's prime minister?"

"It better still be Justin Trudeau, or else I

might welcome slipping into a coma."

Daniel chuckled. "How are you feeling?"

Cole groaned. "Okay, I guess. Can I have more Tylenol?"

"Sure." Daniel sat up and reached for the bottle and water he'd left on the nightstand. "What hurts? Still your head?"

"Yeah. It's a bit better, though. My hand is throbbing."

Daniel slipped his hand under Cole's neck and helped him swallow the tablets. Then he put a note in his phone of the time and dosage, adding in the dose from the middle of the night too. "One last question: How much of a douche was I to you when our parents were married?"

Cole blinked at him blearily, then rubbed his eyes with his right hand. "You were fine. Don't worry about it."

"Ugh. That means I was a *total* douche, doesn't it? Was I ever nice to you?" He curled on his side under the duvet.

After a few moments of silence, Cole said, "It's not like you were *mean*. You just ignored me most of the time. I get it. You were pissed you had to move into our house and change schools. But after you and Trevor got together and came out, you were less angry."

That sounded about right. The thought of Trevor's bright smile and shaggy blond hair were a dull knife between his ribs even after so many years. Especially when he remembered how thrilling it had been when they'd first kissed and made out in the locker room after one-on-one practice on the rink. Trevor had seemed perfect for him. It had been four years before Daniel realized how wrong he'd been.

"I'm sorry I wasn't nicer. And I'm sorry I didn't help you. You know, about being queer."

"But you did. It's because of you I figured it out." In the pale dawn light, Cole's cheeks flushed. "I mean because you came out and were so bold. So brave."

Daniel snorted. "Trust me, I wasn't as brave as I seemed."

"It took guts to come out in high school. You and Trevor were so out and proud and all that. Once you decided to do something, you did it all the way."

"I guess. I was terrified at first when we walked down the hall at school holding hands. But aside from a few jerks, everyone took it in stride. Even our parents did. My mom joined PFLAG, like, the next day."

Cole smiled. "That's Claudia for you. And yeah, my dad's been cool. My mom was great." His eyes took on a faraway, pensive look, but before Daniel could offer any clumsy sympathy, Cole rubbed his face and said, "Anyway. Don't worry about the past. You're more than making up for any douchiness now since I'm crashing your getaway. Although I guess I've got lots of company in the crashing department."

Daniel grimaced. "Indeed."

"I think you might have to schedule some term meetings in the new year," Cole teased.

"Now there's a tempting thought." The house was still and silent, but soon enough he could wake up Justin and the others and send them packing. "I'll let them sleep a little while longer, and then they're out of here."

"Yeah? I wasn't sure if you'd have second thoughts once you cooled off." He quickly added, "Not that you shouldn't be mad. Or that you should have second thoughts."

"Like you said, once I make a decision, I don't back down. They can go party somewhere else. Melanie, Paul, and Jean-Luc seem cool, but I still want them all gone."

"Uh-huh. Totally. So it'll just be you and me, I guess."

Daniel hadn't really thought about it. "I guess so." Strangely enough, the thought of spending the week with Cole sent a bloom of warmth through his chest. "Is that okay with you?"

"Of course!" Cole's voice was doing that squeaky thing. He cleared his throat. "I mean, yeah. Sure. This place is amazing. I can't wait to see it in the daylight."

"Speaking of which…" Daniel threw back the duvet and went to the window, tugging up his silk pajama bottoms where they'd slipped down to his hips and scratching his chest under his T-shirt. He pulled the curtains open, blinking into the light. For a moment, he stared in puzzlement at the unending wall of whiteness. Then his stomach dropped.

"Oh, fuck me."

ARMS CROSSED, DANIEL stood by the massive windows on the side of the chalet facing the driveway. Beside him, Justin shifted nervously and said, "I don't think the minivan will even make it to the road until the plow comes. Jean-Luc's mom only has all-seasons on it, not snow tires. Crazy, I know, but she hardly drives in winter, apparently."

At least Justin seemed a little remorseful in the light of day—and now that he was sober. He peered up at the sky, which still unleashed a steady snowfall. "It doesn't look like it's stopping any time soon."

Behind them, Melanie said, "My weather app says snow all day. A hundred percent chance. We might have to stay with you and your brother if we can't get out of here."

"He's not my brother," Daniel and Cole said in unison.

Cole joined them at the windows, still in his flannel PJ bottoms but with a green sweatshirt on now. It was roomy enough for his cast, the orange and white sticking out, his fingertips barely showing.

Jean-Luc approached. "I just called every hotel in Tremblant on the landline. They're all full."

Unsurprising since it was Christmas vacation. Daniel gritted his teeth. "I guess you guys are staying until tomorrow."

Jean-Luc said, "Thanks, Dan." He glared at Justin. "We really had no idea we weren't invited."

"It's Daniel," Cole said. "He hates being called Dan."

"*Merde!*" Jean-Luc shook his head. "I forgot."

Daniel gave Cole a little smile, then said, "It's okay. After a while, I stopped fighting it at work."

Justin sidled closer. "Should I call you Danny instead?"

"No." Daniel gave him what he thought of as a full Death-Star glare.

With a big sigh, Justin actually *pouted*. "I said I'm sorry. Are you going to be grumpy all day?"

Melanie said, "Dude, I don't blame you. But hey, let me wake up Paul and we can make breakfast. His French toast is to die for."

Daniel groaned. "Shit. I was going to head into

the village today to buy food."

"No worries! Paul and I brought challah and maple syrup. And bacon, of course," she added eagerly. "And the cupboards have a lot of staples, and there are chicken fingers and burgers someone must have left behind. Jean-Luc brought a bunch of chips too. Oh, and there's a whole jar of popcorn, and plenty of oil. We definitely won't starve. I did a mental inventory last night. I really like food."

Daniel exhaled. There was no sense in being pissed at her when she was trying so hard to be kind. If she, Paul, and Jean-Luc were lying about not knowing they hadn't been invited, they were pretty good actors.

He said, "Cool. Thanks, Melanie. If you guys could make breakfast, that would be great."

"We're on it." She gave him a thumbs-up and scurried off.

"You know, we can still have fun." Justin slid his hand up Daniel's arm.

Jerking away, Daniel headed for the kitchen. "We're definitely never having *that* kind of fun again." His skin crawled.

Bleary, barrel-chested Mike, shuffling downstairs, muttered, "Never say never. Justin will do anything to win a bet." He ran a hand through his mop of brown hair.

Daniel skidded to a stop, his socks sliding a

few inches on the wood. The sticky, itchy ball of mortification that had taken up residence in his gut the night before spread its fingers wide. He turned to face Justin, who was shooting eye-daggers at Mike at the bottom of the stairs. Cole and Jean-Luc watched from the windows.

Daniel gritted out, "What does that mean?"

With a careless roll of his eyes, Justin answered, "Louise bet me I couldn't bag you. I told her I already did in the parking lot, but she's dubious."

Icy rage slithered down Daniel's spine. "Bag me."

"You know, take that giant stick up your ass and replace it with my dick? Or you could fuck me." He waved a hand. "Whichever."

It had been a *bet*.

Just when Daniel thought he couldn't be more humiliated. His face burned, and he wished the hardwood floor would crack open and swallow him whole.

Mel and Paul descended the stairs, and Mel asked, "What's going on?"

Justin opened his stupid, ugly, hateful mouth, but then Cole said, "Daniel, I feel sick. Can you take me upstairs?"

"Oh, you poor thing!" Mel fussed over Cole as Daniel forced his feet to move. Left, right, left right. He grasped Cole's good arm and led him up the stairs, glad for the warmth under his fingers, ice and fire battling in Daniel's veins. From below, Justin snickered and voices murmured, and Daniel wanted to scream.

He didn't. He walked Cole back into the master bedroom, closing the door behind them. Managing to keep his voice even, he asked, "Are you nauseous?"

"Yes, but only because of that piece of shit downstairs."

Daniel exhaled, the ice melting in a rush of gratitude, embarrassment still simmering. "Thanks for getting me out of there. God, you must think I'm pathetic."

Cole's thin brows drew together. "No, I think he's a massive loser. A ginormous one. Humongous. Monumental. Colossal. Mammoth." He seemed to ponder. "Whopping. Gigantic. Supersized loser."

A little laugh bubbled up, and Daniel took a deep breath. "Thanks."

"I play Words with Friends a lot."

Daniel's smile faded. "I don't know how I let myself get snowed by him."

"A snake like that? I bet he can be pretty charming when he wants to be. And it's easy to see what you want to see. Especially…"

After a few moments, Daniel asked, "What?"

"Especially if you're lonely."

He wanted to argue, even opened his mouth and sucked in air, but the denial wouldn't come. "I really am pathetic."

"No, he is. Do you want me to list some other synonyms to describe how truly lame that jerk is?

"It's okay. But thanks."

"You know, I think there's a *Star Wars* marathon on this week. They're showing the movies over and over on TBS." He nodded to the flat-screen TV on the wall across from the bed. "We could check out where they're at in the cycle."

It sounded like the best idea ever proposed in the history of the world. But Cole didn't need to shut himself away to keep Daniel company. "The doctor said you didn't have to stay in bed."

"But she didn't say I couldn't." He flopped back onto the mattress, then grimaced. "Note to self: still need to ease into things."

Daniel propped up several pillows behind Cole, then turned on the TV. Cole said, "Uh, you might want to keep a pillow for yourself."

"Nah. Headboard's padded. I'm good. Are you hungry?"

"A little?"

There was a tentative knock on the door. Daniel answered it, finding Melanie biting her lip. "Hey. Is Cole okay?"

"Yeah, but I think we're just going to chill in here. He needs to rest, and I'm going to take care of him."

"Totally. I'll make sure we stay quiet downstairs. No music. We'll hang in the hot tub and stay out of your hair. If that's okay?"

"Of course."

Her face creased. "Jean-Luc said something about a bet? We really didn't know about that. I'm sorry, Dan. *Daniel!* Shit, I'm going to get that right. I promise."

"It's okay." He gave her a smile. "I appreciate you trying."

"Do you guys want breakfast? I saw some trays in the kitchen. We can bring it up."

"Thanks. That's really nice of you."

She shook her head, waving him off. "It's the least I can do to make up for that douche. Paul and I are done hanging out with him and his lackeys. Jean-Luc too. We're getting too old for this shit."

She quizzed him and Cole on their breakfast preferences, and Daniel shut the door again. He went to grab his phone from the other side of the bed. He asked Cole, "Is the light too much? Do you want me to close the curtains?"

"I think I'm good. My head really does feel better. I'll let you know if that changes."

"Cool. I think the symptoms can come and go with a concussion." He tapped his phone. "I'd Google it, but the wifi definitely isn't connecting."

He glanced down at his PJs. Normally by this time he'd have worked out, showered, dressed, and would be behind his desk. He tried to connect again. No dice. "It's so weird that I'm not at work right now."

"It's Saturday."

"Oh, right. Well, I'd be working at home."

"Also you're on vacation and your office is closed. Right?"

Familiar irritation sparked. "*Yes*, but there's always something to do."

Cole watched him impassively, apparently not intimidated at all. "Yeah, of course there is. And it'll get done after the holidays. The world won't end."

"I know, I know. I work too much. I care about what I do, okay? It's important to me."

Cole still watched him with a dubious expression. "Yeah, I don't care at *all* about my thesis."

"That's not what I mean."

"Then what do you mean?" Cole asked calmly. "That people who aren't workaholics don't care about their jobs?"

"No! I just…" *Don't have anything else.* "I'm just used to checking my email and staying on top of things so tasks don't pile up. That's all." It sounded weak even to him.

"Well, I guess you'll be CYCing on that front whether you like it or not." Cole smiled tentatively.

The tension released, and Daniel had to laugh. "I guess I will."

Cole nodded to the TV, where lightsabers clashed. "We're in luck. Episode three is almost over, so we're just in time for the movies that don't suck."

Daniel went around to his side of the bed, noticing Cole had put two of the pillows back for him. He got settled and looked at the screen. "Oh, I think Padme's about to die of a broken heart."

Cole huffed. "I hate that. I mean, she just had two babies who need her. And now she dies of a broken heart because of that whiny dickbag Anakin? She was tougher than that."

"*Thank you.* I hate that too."

"And don't get me started on Hayden Christensen's acting in these movies."

Daniel put on a vacant, flat voice, imitating the most famous cringe-worthy line of dialogue. "I don't like sand. It's coarse and rough and irritating and it gets everywhere."

Cole's face lit up as he burst out laughing. "Don't make me laugh too hard! I have a concussion, you know."

Yet as they ate French toast and bacon—Cole insisting his stomach could take it—and watched Princess Leia and R2-D2 huddle, Daniel wanted to make him laugh again and again so he could see the little dimple that creased his left cheek.

"IF YOU'RE HAVING second thoughts we can just stay in here all night," Cole said. "It's fine by me."

Daniel pulled a soft charcoal sweater over his head, tugging it gently to make sure it wasn't wrinkled. "I know, but I want to prove that he doesn't bother me. That I couldn't care less."

"I totally get it."

"You can stay here, though. Rest." Daniel secretly hoped Cole would come downstairs. He'd feel better not being alone. Not that he'd be *alone* with six other people, but… "Seriously, I can handle it."

Cole was still in his PJs and sweatshirt. "I napped enough for today. I'm still pissed I slept through the first half of Empire."

"We'll catch it when it comes around again tomorrow. Or the next day. No rush." They'd have the rest of the week together—a prospect Daniel found increasingly appealing. He could admit his mom was right—he should have reached out to Cole months ago.

The driveway had finally been plowed by an apologetic man in a pickup truck hired by the chalet owners, and the main roads had been cleared. Come the morning, he and Cole would be blissfully alone. Daniel had been awfully tempted to kick the others out the nanosecond the driveway had been scraped clean, but they'd been drinking.

He eyed himself in the long mirror standing in the corner, smoothing down his damp curls. He'd showered and shaved and splashed on cologne. Which was all profoundly stupid, but a spark of pride blazed.

"You look great," Cole said. "Let's do this. Show that dick what he's missing out on."

Head high, Daniel led the way, making sure Cole was okay on the stairs. The others lounged on the leather couches near the fireplace. They'd apparently had enough hot-tubbing for the moment and wore sweats and T-shirts. This was going to be just fine. He'd show Justin he wasn't bothered or hurt at all. He'd—

"Dare," Melanie said. "I guess."

Daniel's stomach dropped. He'd apparently be joining in a game of truth or dare. He couldn't retreat now that everyone had spotted him. With Cole at his side, he walked on and took a seat like there was nothing the matter at all. Nope. Nothing the matter here. Cold and dead inside and utterly unruffled.

"Hey!" Jean-Luc grinned. "Feeling better, Cole? You guys want beer?"

"Much," Cole answered. "Thanks. And no, I can't drink for a few days until I'm sure my head's clear."

"You're going to have to put up with Mr. Grumpy sober?" Justin winced. "*Vaya con dios.*"

Mike groaned. "Enough, dude. You lost the bet. Deal. Are we playing or what?" He gulped from his bottle of beer.

"I dare you to kiss me," Paul said to Melanie, who sat on the floor between the coffee table and the couch, leaning back between his knees.

She rolled her eyes and lifted her face for a peck. Then she said, "Cole, you want to go?"

Daniel was about to insist that Cole was under no obligation to play these reindeer games, but Cole lifted his cast and said, "I can't really do many dares right now. Truth, I guess."

Justin's blue eyes gleamed, his expression one of faux innocence. "Just how big of a boner did you have for Daniel when you were kids?"

Cole stammered, going beet red. Melanie, Paul, and Jean-Luc groaned, while Louise shrieked with laughter and Mike chugged more beer. Rage slammed through Daniel like a tidal wave. How *dare* Justin pick on Cole? Daniel had never been one for violence, but the idea of punching Justin's smug face burned.

He managed to contain it, gritting out, "Don't be ridiculous."

Melanie shook her head. "You're so gross, Justin."

Chugging his beer, Justin shrugged. "You're the ones who keep insisting you're not brothers."

"We're not! That doesn't mean we'd ever…" Daniel grimaced, furious denial surging. He and Cole would never get together! They weren't brothers, but it would still be inappropriate as hell.

Wouldn't it?

As Justin howled with laughter, images of being with Cole flashed through Daniel's mind. Kissing Cole, touching his skin, pressing their bodies together—

*What the fuck is wrong with me?*

Paul said to Justin, "I really don't know why you and your minions have to be such turds. Didn't I tell you, Mel? No hot tub is worth this."

Daniel's mind spun. He should have been horrified to think of Cole that way—or at the very least, unmoved. Yet his balls tingled, the fire of his initial denial transforming. It wasn't possible. He hadn't felt a connection to anyone in years, and now…with *Cole*?

He glanced at Cole, whose face was creased with what looked like pain. Pushing aside his confusion, Daniel asked him, "Do you need more Tylenol?"

Cole shook his head and dropped his gaze as Jean-Luc said, "My turn. Dare me."

Mike belched and suggested, "Strip naked, go outside, and make a snow angel."

"Is that all you've got?" Jean-Luc rolled his eyes as he stood. He took off all his clothes, leaving them in a pile.

Daniel tried desperately to focus on Jean-Luc's antics instead of the entirely inappropriate bolt of desire for Cole. It was crazy to feel that. He was just all worked up and confused because of Justin.

Right?

Everyone got up to watch from the windows as Jean-Luc skipped outside, and Daniel followed, forcing a laugh as Jean-Luc flopped into the snow, yelping as he flapped his arms and legs. Cole's smile was strained, and Daniel leaned close to him.

*Be normal. Everything is normal.*

He asked Cole, "Sure you don't need more Tylenol?"

Cole kept his gaze on Jean-Luc, who was now sprinting along the porch and back inside. "Nah. Thanks." His voice was even.

*Everything's fine. Totally normal. Nothing to see here but the naked dude I work with.*

Jean-Luc shook his body and hurried to the fireplace, apparently utterly unashamed by his nudity. He took a towel from Melanie and narrowed his gaze at Mike. "Your turn. Truth or dare?"

Only a fool would choose dare at that point, so of course Mike lifted his chin and said, "Dare."

Daniel had to confess he didn't mind at all

when Mike had to shave off his chest hair, whining the whole time.

"HEY, BABE."

Daniel groaned internally at the kitchen sink where he was rinsing dishes. The others had gone back into the hot tub, and Cole had retreated upstairs to rest. Daniel just wanted to clean up and join him.

*Because I want to make sure he's okay. Not because I want to jump him or anything.*

Apparently he'd have to deal with more of Justin's bullshit first. He turned and affected a bored expression as Justin sidled closer, a gleam in his eyes, wearing only a towel wrapped around his hips and possibly his teeny-tiny Speedo underneath. Justin displayed his lean muscles and ripped abs, his chest puffed out like he was on a catwalk.

Daniel couldn't believe he'd ever found Justin anything but absolutely repellent. He was never CYCing to that degree again. Nope. His cadence was just fine.

His lower back jammed against the counter, and while he could have shoved Justin away, he didn't want to show that he was bothered at all. He waited to see what game Justin was playing now.

"You know, we could still have a lot of fun tonight." Justin dropped his hand to Daniel's crotch and squeezed.

"But we won't." He felt nothing but contempt. "I need to go up and check on Cole, so if you're done here…" He made a flicking motion with his hand.

Spine stiffening, Justin let go. Then his face twisted and he practically bared his too-white teeth. "Oh yes, go check on your precious Cole. Who is totally into you, by the way. I know you're retarded when it comes to sex, but—"

"Don't use that word, asshole."

"What, 'sex'? You really *are* a prude. You should know that when we hooked up in your car, I hadn't worked so hard to give a guy a blow job in…ever."

He shrugged. "Not my fault your technique is lacking."

Justin jolted as if he'd been slapped. "I'll have you know my technique is *legendary!*"

Ignoring that, Daniel's mind caught up to the rest of what Justin had said before. "And you've been smoking too much grass if you think Cole—"

"Would jump on your dick in a heartbeat if you let him? Trust me, Danny. You know, I could help you poor guys out. The three of us could have *such* a good time. Loosen up already."

Now Daniel did shove him away, jagged-edged

memories of Trevor spinning through his mind. "Fuck you." Chest tight, he concentrated on keeping his voice even. *I'm cold and dead inside. I'm not supposed to get upset.* "You're leaving in the morning if you have to walk to town."

With that, he stalked past Justin out of the kitchen, the buzz of anger in his head blocking out whatever taunts Justin was hurling after him. At the foot of the stairs, he met Jean-Luc, who curled his lip scornfully as he glared toward the kitchen.

"We'll leave tomorrow for sure. We've all had enough of him. Well, maybe not Louise and Mike, but they can have him. You know, maybe we can hang out sometime in the new year? You're a good guy, Dan. *Daniel.* Sorry."

Daniel exhaled a long breath and gave him a little smile. "It's okay. And that would be cool."

Mel called from the doorway to the hot tub enclosure. "Guys, come taste this."

His muscles unclenching bit by bit, Daniel followed Jean-Luc over, hoping Justin would see how unbothered Daniel was. *That's me. Completely unfazed. Cold and dead inside.*

Mel held out a beer bottle, and Jean-Luc said, "We've tasted Moosehead before."

She rolled her eyes. "Yeah, but I added something."

Jean-Luc took the bottle and lifted it to his lips. His eyebrows shot up, and he took another sip. "Is that...maple syrup? It's actually good!" He held out the bottle to Daniel.

Raising his hands, Daniel said, "I'm good. That sounds disgusting."

Mel called, "Cole, how about you? Want to try my new beer recipe?"

Heart skipping, Daniel turned to see Cole about to go into the kitchen. Cole answered, "I still can't drink right now, but thanks!" He disappeared around the bend.

Shit, was Justin still in there? Daniel hurried after Cole. He wouldn't put it past Justin to—

"I tried to help you out, sweetie. I suggested we do a three-way, but Dan just isn't into you at all."

"I swear to God, if you don't shut your fucking mouth, you're sleeping in the snow," Daniel roared. Justin jumped, spinning around and shrinking back gratifyingly.

Justin lifted his hands. "Okay, okay. So touchy." To Cole he added, "Don't say I didn't try, sugar!" He skirted around the island and disappeared.

Cole stood frozen by the fridge. After a few beats, he asked, "Are you okay?"

Fists clenched, blood rushed in Daniel's ears. "Yeah," he bit out. "Do you need something? More water?"

Trevor's voice echoed through his mind: *"Threesomes are hot. Come on, loosen up."*

Cole opened the fridge. "I wanted a little juice." He took out the OJ container.

Daniel hurried over to unscrew the cap and pour him a glass. Cole took it and said, "Thanks. I'll just…" He motioned toward the stairs with an awkward wave.

Nodding, Daniel followed. The sooner he went to sleep, the sooner morning could come and Justin would be gone.

# Chapter Six

INHALING AND EXHALING forcefully, Daniel shook his head, leaning against the closed bedroom door. "I can't believe I ever thought for a second I liked that guy," he muttered. "*Threesome.* He should get together with Trevor."

Cole had been about to switch on the lamp, but he froze, hand in midair. Would Daniel talk to him, or should he leave him be?

Daniel snapped up straight as if just realizing what he'd said. He strode toward the bathroom. "I'm going to have a shower. You need anything?"

"What happened with Trevor?" After a few moments of silence, Daniel hovering in the bathroom doorway, silhouetted by the light beyond, Cole added, "I know you don't want to talk about it. But maybe you should?" Cole was definitely curious, but there truly seemed to be a well of pain there that hunched Daniel's shoulders and haunted his eyes.

Daniel turned and leaned against the door jamb. His face was in shadow. Cole sat on the end of the bed facing him. Giving him some distance, but listening. Waiting.

After what felt like an eternity, Daniel quietly asked, "What do you remember about Trevor?"

"Hmm. Well, after you and your mom moved in with us, you had to switch schools. You joined the hockey team and met Trevor. You guys hung out a lot. Then that one night you brought him to dinner and came out. School ended, and you both went to Western in the fall. Claudia moved out just before Thanksgiving, and even though I saw her sometimes, I never saw you again. Until now. Obviously."

Cole wiped his palms on his flannel PJ bottoms. He wasn't sure why he was nervous—it was Daniel's story to tell.

Daniel crossed his arms, the warm light from the bathroom outlining his left side—broad shoulder, then narrowing down to his slim hip and long leg. "Right. So things with Trev were great for a few years. I was so in love with him. I felt like… Like he really *got* me. We could finish each other's sentences. That kind of shit. You know what I mean?"

"Theoretically. I dated guys in university, but I never felt like that." *Never felt the way I do for you.*

"It's a real rush. Like I said, everything was great. At least I thought it was." He was silent a few moments. "We had an apartment off-campus. Never lived on campus. In our fourth year, there was a big dorm party Trevor wanted to go to. We usually hung out at the pub and stuff, so it was weird that he was so insistent on going. But I wanted to make him happy, so I went."

Cole realized he was holding his breath. He exhaled and murmured, "Okay."

"Anyway, we got pretty loaded, and it was fun and all. I was ready to go home and crash, but there was this guy Trevor knew. Alex. Alex said he had vodka in his room, and Trevor wanted to do a couple shots. So I went."

"To make Trevor happy."

"Yeah." Daniel swallowed audibly, a sort of click in the stillness of the room. If the others were making noise, it didn't penetrate the walls. The curtains were drawn, and it was like they were in a little cave.

Cole felt like he had to whisper. "What happened?"

"God, it's so stupid. You're going to think it's nothing and that I'm a massive drama queen. Maybe I am."

"No, of course—"

"Long story short, Trevor wanted to have a threesome with Alex. I said yes, because he wanted it. It was fine. And I figured Trevor would get it out of his system, and we could just go back to normal. To being…us."

Cole winced. "But that didn't happen."

Daniel's laugh was humorless. "Nope. So we had more threesomes. We went to a bathhouse. Trevor wanted sex with all these random people, and I just *didn't*. And it's not like there's anything wrong with that." He groaned. "I probably sound like such a judgmental asshole. Threesomes and anonymous hookups and all that are totally great for other people. If it floats your boat, go for it."

*Was that a question? Should I answer?* "It's not really my thing either. But yeah, to each their own and all that." Cole could sense Daniel's laser gaze in the darkness. He still leaned in the doorway, his face shadowed.

After a few moments, Daniel asked, "Are you just saying that to make me feel better?"

"No! I mean, I get turned on by hot guys, and I've had some bathroom hand jobs and stuff. Fucked some guys on the first date. But I want more than that now." *I want you. I've always wanted you.*

"I know most people can get super turned on by strangers, but I never have. When Justin pursued me and blew me, I really wasn't that into it, but I wanted to make him happy." He snorted. "And I was trying to CYC. So he sucked me and it was fine and everything. I…" He shook his head. "I'm sorry, you don't want to hear all this crap. I should save it for my shrink. Or actually get a shrink first, I guess."

"No, I want to listen. I mean, if you want to tell me. No pressure."

Daniel's intent gaze made Cole's skin go hot. "I don't know why I'm unloading all this."

"Because Justin's dickishness stirred up a bunch of feelings?"

"I guess so. I'm supposed to be cold and dead inside."

"Wait, what? Why is that?"

Daniel waved his hand, cutting through the light from the bathroom. "It's a joke I have with my friend Pam. How I can be…stoic a lot of the time. And…a workaholic."

Cole kept his tone light. "Admitting it is the first step."

"Yeah, yeah," Daniel grumbled, but there was no heat to it. After a few moments, he said, "I don't know what's wrong with me. I'm usually much more…contained."

A thrill whipped through Cole at he was peeking beneath the mask. "It's okay to come undone sometimes."

"I guess. Lucky you, huh? We haven't seen each other in ten years and now you get a front-row seat to my nervous breakdown. I'm a workaholic freak who doesn't like casual sex the way I'm supposed to."

"You are *not* a freak. Fuck anyone who says you're *supposed* to like anything."

"But I'm missing some element that other people have. Especially guys. It's like, I'm supposed to want to go clubbing and have orgies, and I just…don't."

"There's nothing wrong with that. I have a friend who's demi, and there's nothing wrong with her."

"Demi?"

"Demisexual. Basically she's only really attracted to someone if she cares about them."

Daniel pushed off the wall, taking a step toward the bed. He stopped. "I didn't know there was a name for that."

"Oh yeah, there's a name for everything now."

"Huh." He came to sit on Cole's left. "I didn't realize that was a thing. But it's not as if I'm not attracted to people. I mean, I can appreciate a good-looking guy. Admire his body and think that he's hot. I like looking at Chris Hemsworth and his abs. But I don't want to *actually* bang him. Not that that's the only thing standing between me and Chris Hemsworth."

Cole laughed. "I know what you mean."

"So do I fit this demisexual thing?"

"I don't think there's only one right way to be

demi. It sounds like you might identify with it, but I can't tell you yes or no. That's up to you. I can ask my friend Julia if she has links to any good blogs if you want?"

"Thanks. That would be cool." Daniel was silent a minute as they sat there, and Cole could practically hear his mind working. Then Daniel blurted, "I really like sex! I'm not a prude."

"I know. I believe you. It's okay. It really is." He could not think much more closely on Daniel and sex, his belly tightening with a bolt of desire. He ached to hold Daniel close and comfort him, but part of him—the part that had been horny for Daniel for years—wanted so much more.

*Rein it in, asshole. Not now. Not that there ever will be a right time, but it definitely isn't now.*

"I can't believe I'm talking about this." Daniel rubbed his face. "I really am losing it."

"I think we should all be talking about it more. It sucks that we feel this pressure from society to conform. Like, all gay men are supposed to be promiscuous? Fuck that. Gay men are not the Borg. No one is. Everyone gets to be who they are."

"This demi thing is blowing my mind. I thought I was weird all these years."

"Well, you are, but not because of this." As soon as the words were out, Cole cringed internally. Was joking really the right approach?

But Daniel snorted and said, "Yeah, yeah," as he elbowed him. Cole sucked in a breath, pain radiating from his upper arm down to his hand. "Shit!" Daniel exclaimed. "Are you okay?"

He pressed his lips together, inhaling. "Mmm-hmm." Opening his mouth, he blew out the breath, relaxing. "It's just all a little sensitive. I'm okay."

"You sure?" Daniel's hand hovered over Cole's shoulder, as if he was afraid to touch and hurt him more. Cole was dying to tell him to go ahead, but he resisted.

"Yep." Time to focus back on Daniel. "So, about Trevor. Obviously you guys broke up in the end. What went down? Unless you don't want to talk about it anymore."

Only an inch separated them, and Cole wished he could rest his palm on Daniel's thigh. Just to ground him. But even if Cole's hand wasn't broken, he wouldn't do it anyway.

The image of Daniel's face after Justin's taunts about them hooking up was seared into Cole's mind. Wide-eyed shock and fury, and a grimace of what had to be disgust. Daniel had made it clear he was outraged at the mere idea, and Cole wasn't about to cross any lines—especially given the story Daniel was telling. Sounded like crossing lines was Trevor's specialty, and Cole would *not* be that guy.

Daniel was still silent, and Cole added, "Seriously, you don't need to tell me."

"I…" His shoulders relaxed a fraction. "I guess it's good to talk about it. I know you won't go blabbing. I trust you."

Cole's heart skipped, and he watched Daniel's profile from the corner of his eye, the bathroom light on his face. "I trust you too."

When Daniel looked at him with a tiny smile tugging at his lips and a dark curl hanging over his forehead, Cole thought his heart might swell too big for his body and explode. As a kid, he'd been in love with Daniel yet hadn't really known him. Or known what love really was. Maybe he still didn't, but his gut told him this was it.

Which meant he was royally screwed.

Daniel turned his head back to stare off toward the bathroom, his gaze unfocused, and Cole looked forward as well. He waited. There was something more to the story—something he had a feeling was going to make him hate Trevor Chartrand with every fiber of his being.

When Daniel spoke, his deep voice was steady. "So I went along with the threesomes and stuff because I figured if Trevor needed that, then I'd do what it took to make him happy. Satisfied. We still had sex just the two of us, and I didn't feel like anything had changed there. Then I found out Trevor had been hooking up with guys behind my back pretty much since we went away to school."

"That asshole!" Cole cleared his throat and lowered his voice. "Sorry."

"Don't be. He is an asshole. He cheated on me for years, then figured if he brought me into experimenting with other guys, I'd be converted or something. Like I'd see that monogamy isn't possible. That it's only for straight people. That kind of bullshit. He made it my fault, like…" Dropping his head, Daniel's voice went husky. "Like there was something wrong with me. For a long time, I guess I thought there was."

Forgetting his cast, Cole reached out abortively. With a grunt of frustration, he got up and sat on Daniel's other side, taking hold of his shoulder. "There is *nothing* wrong with you. Trevor's an asshole and he can go fuck himself."

Daniel's eyes gleamed in the half-darkness, and he swiped at them, laughing. "But how do you really feel? Don't hold back."

Cole laughed too. "I could go on. There are some extremely colorful expletives I could use."

"Thanks, man." He took a long breath and blew it out. "I haven't really talked about all that stuff. Sorry for dumping it on you. I'm supposed to be taking care of you, not the other way around."

Cole squeezed his shoulder. "I'm not a kid anymore." He smoothed his palm behind Daniel's neck, longing to run his fingers through the ends of the soft curls. Instead he slapped him on the back like a buddy would and dropped his hand. "We can take care of each other."

Shattering glass echoed up from downstairs, followed by Mel screaming, "For fuck's sake, Justin!"

In unison, Cole and Daniel huffed. Cole said, "Speaking of people who can go fuck themselves."

"Indeed."

They sat in silence for a minute. There was so much Cole wanted to say, but he didn't know where to start. Instead, he said, "I feel kind of gross. I don't think I'm ready to attempt a shower yet with this thing, but I think a sponge bath is in order. Can you help me?"

Daniel blinked at him, mouth opening and closing. "You want me to give you a sponge bath?"

"No!" Cole's cheeks went hot, and he was glad it was probably too dark to see his blush. "I just mean if you could unscrew the bottle of body wash and help me take off my sweatshirt? I tried earlier and almost strangled myself." He forced a laugh that was too high-pitched.

"Oh, right. Totally!" Daniel sprang up and hurried into the bathroom.

Cole followed. "Sorry to be a pain."

"No, not at all!" Daniel kept his head down as he turned on the taps at the sink. "Do you want to just do it here with a washcloth or whatever?"

"Yeah. That's great."

In the mirror, Cole could glimpse the faint rosy hue on Daniel's cheeks. Clearly Daniel was embarrassed after his confessions, and Cole wanted to say something to reassure him, but would probably just make it worse. He went to the floating shelves on the far wall and picked out a facecloth from the piles of plush, navy-blue towels.

Daniel had plugged one of the sinks and apparently squeezed in half the bottle of body wash given the mountain of bubbles forming. He turned to Cole and motioned with his hand. "So you need help with stuff?"

Cole dropped the facecloth on the counter by the filling sink. "Thanks. If you can just…" He held his right arm up over his head, holding still as Daniel pulled up the hem of Cole's sweatshirt, his fingertips brushing Cole's ribs.

*It's okay. I don't need to breathe.*

His pulse thudded, and he stayed absolutely still as Daniel freed his right arm, eased the sweatshirt over Cole's head, then peeled it down his left arm over the cast as though he was dealing with fragile glass. They were only a couple inches apart, and Daniel's breath skimmed over Cole's face.

Gripping the sweatshirt, Daniel looked up, and Cole's lungs spasmed as he exhaled sharply, going lightheaded. Daniel's parted lips trembled the slightest bit, and emotion shone from his beautiful hazel-brown eyes. Cole scrambled to identify what the emotion was, because for a moment he'd thought it was lust.

And that was impossible.

He croaked, "Are you okay?" Daniel was probably just freaking out after revealing so many truths about Trevor and everything.

Backing up, Daniel nodded. He folded the sweatshirt and placed it on the counter, his gaze skittering away. "You good now?"

"Uh-huh. Thanks." He'd become adept already at tugging his PJ bottoms up and down. Yep, he was *great*.

When Daniel closed the door behind him, Cole sagged against the counter. It was decidedly less great that Cole was falling hopelessly in love, especially since—barring some kind of Christmas miracle—there was zero chance of his feelings being returned.

# Chapter Seven

THE MINIVAN'S TAILLIGHTS glowed red, sunlight glinting off the metal roof before it disappeared around the bend. Cole joined Daniel at the windows, and they sighed in unison, then laughed. Daniel's belly somersaulted. They were alone.

"Hallelujah," Cole said. He was still shirtless, his PJs hanging low on his hips. Daniel stared at the hair under his navel, leading down below the waistband.

Forcing his gaze up, he asked, "How are you feeling?"

After yawning and arching his back, Cole nodded. "Pretty good. I slept way better without you waking me up every two hours."

Daniel smiled. "You know what? I slept way better not having to wake you up."

"Huh. What are the odds?" Cole scratched his

stubbly cheeks, smiling. While Daniel usually shaved religiously, he'd decided to let it go too. CYC and all that.

They stood in blissful silence, taking in the snow-capped trees soaring toward the blue sky, the Laurentians rising across the lake to the right.

Daniel had woken to find he'd drawn close to Cole in the night, only a few inches between them on the big bed. Those same inches were all that separated them now, their shoulders almost brushing.

He still couldn't believe he'd confessed the truth about Trevor—about himself—to Cole. Maybe he should have been embarrassed to tell those things, but he'd felt...safe. Something about Cole comforted him in a way he didn't understand. His instincts told him Cole had his back.

Maybe it was because they'd known each other before, but Daniel had never met anyone he trusted so quickly—not even Trevor. Cole hadn't judged or ridiculed him. He'd stood by his side for the whole ugly retelling of it. Now the tug toward Cole grew stronger by the minute. Did Cole feel it too, or was he simply being a good friend? Brotherly, even?

Daniel wished he could text Pam: *After being cold and dead inside for six years, I might be coming back to life. Send help.*

He thought about what Cole had said about it

being okay to come undone sometimes. That was what it felt like—an unraveling, all his tightly coiled and controlled emotions spilling out in a hot mess. Apparently he was CYCing all over the damn place, whether he liked it or not.

"What do you want to do first?" Cole asked.

Daniel took a breath and forced away his crazy thoughts. *I'm good. Everything's fine. I'm still me. I'm in control.* He kept his tone light. "Honestly? I know it's a waste of water, but drain and refill that hot tub."

Needing something to do with his hands, he rolled up the sleeves of his black Henley. Before he'd dressed, he'd ridiculously debated between his shirts and which went better with his jeans, as if he was going on some kind of *date*.

"After Justin, that water is a biohazard. I'll allow it. You do that, and I'll see if I can make some one-handed breakfast. Oh. Maybe we should call Claudia? She's probably worried if she's texted with no replies."

"Shit! You're right." He grabbed the cordless, then paused, looking at the number pad. "I'll have to get her number from my cell. The only one I know by heart now is my own. And 911."

Cole laughed. "Same."

Once Daniel had the number, he waited for his mom to pick up. It went to voicemail. "Hey, Mom. It's me and Cole. We're calling from the chalet's landline since we're not getting any wifi or cell service. We're good. Cole's feeling a lot better. Enjoy Mexico. Love you." He hung up and said to Cole, "Okay, hopefully that'll hold her and she won't call back every day to check on us."

"I have my doubts, to be honest."

Daniel laughed. "Same."

Once the hot tub was refilled with the cover back on, the water slowly heating, Daniel joined Cole in the kitchen, the wood cold beneath his bare feet. "What have we got?"

"Frozen blueberry waffles a previous guest left behind and a desperate need to go grocery shopping. Can you unscrew the maple syrup bottle? I tried, but it's sticky." He rubbed at his belly where he'd likely been trying to brace the bottle, then licked the pad of his index finger, his pink tongue darting out.

When he met Daniel's gaze, Daniel jerked, realizing he'd been staring.

"Are you okay?" Cole asked.

"Uh-huh. Here." Heart thumping, he came around the island and opened the syrup, busying himself straightening up the kitchen as the waffles toasted.

"Maybe we could decorate the tree."

"Huh? Oh, right." Daniel had forgotten the fresh Christmas tree standing in the living room. "You want to?"

"Sure. Why not?" Cole smiled crookedly, jumping a little as the waffles popped up, then blushing.

Daniel cut Cole's waffle for him, and they ate while two more toasted. It was all so strangely domestic and should have been uncomfortable and weird, but somehow…wasn't.

After breakfast, they opened the boxes of decorations—colorful balls and glittery ornaments of all shapes and sizes. The chalet owners had left a hand-scrawled note on the top box:

*You said you celebrated Christmas, so we thought you'd enjoy a tree with all the trimmings. Happy holidays!*

Cole pulled out strings of neatly stored, colored lights that were wrapped around plastic frames to keep them untangled. "These hosts really thought of everything, huh?"

"They are getting a five-star review, that's for sure. Well, aside from the wifi, but maybe that's for the best."

He still experienced a bolt of panic when he thought of not being able to check his work email, but Martin had made it clear everyone was to take a break. Blah, blah, work-life balance.

*Look at me. Balancing like a mofo.*

As Cole attempted to unwrap the lights with his right hand, sticking out his tongue adorably in concentration, Daniel resisted the urge to offer help. Instead he went to the stereo, preemptively turning down the volume knob before pressing power so he didn't blow the speakers. Fucking Justin. Daniel hadn't been so glad to see the back of someone since…

Well, no. Despite how it ended with Trevor, part of Daniel would always love him. He wasn't sure he ever wanted to see him again, but he couldn't hate Trevor. Justin, on the other hand… He thought about going back to work in January and groaned.

"Hmm?" Cole was still intent on the lights, spreading them out on the pine floor.

"Just thinking that I wish I didn't have to see Justin again at work. We have an open concept, but at least the designers are on another floor."

"I'm just saying, I think a term meeting is in his future."

Daniel laughed and poked at the stereo. "He's not in my group, so it's not up to me. But yeah, not really looking forward to seeing him again ever."

"So, wait—you don't have an office? It's all open?"

"Luckily for me, my VP insisted HR have enclosures since we have to have confidential meetings with staff. The offices are all glass-fronted, but I'll take them over working in the ball pit."

"Ball pit? Like for kids?"

"People literally sit in there with their laptops. I can't even." He pressed another button, and low music sounded. "Ah. The satellite radio works, at least. No cell network or wifi, but I'll take Sirius." After hunting around, he tuned it to a holiday station, where Elton John invited them to step into Christmas. "Is this too lame?" he asked Cole.

"Two queers decorating a Christmas tree to Elton John? I think it's perfect."

As they wrapped the lights and hung ornaments, Daniel did too.

WHILE COLE FINISHED hanging silver foil icicles with painstaking precision, Daniel did a grocery run, and the day somehow passed by in a blink.

They sprawled on the couch and watched the original *X-Men* that night by the light of their newly decorated Christmas tree, eating the macaroni and cheese with Panko topping that Daniel had made. He'd figured macaroni would be easy enough for Cole to manage on his own, and he was right.

The Christmas lights outside matched the tree, glowing blue, green, yellow, red, pink, and orange. Fresh snow drifted down beyond the wide walls of windows, and Daniel stoked the wood fire, managing to keep it going all evening.

Cole nodded off before the end of the movie, and Daniel considered leaving him on the huge couch with a blanket. But in the end, he gave him a shake, and they shuffled upstairs and into bed.

It wasn't until Daniel was almost asleep, Cole breathing deeply beside him, that he realized neither of them had thought of Cole moving to one of the other bedrooms.

THE NEXT MORNING, Cole was stir crazy and asked to see the village, so they joined the crowd along the main street, a pedestrian thoroughfare jammed with high-end boutiques, restaurants, and various shops. The ski hills rose in the distance, little people zigzagging their way down, the chair lifts ferrying skiers to the top in a constant loop.

The colorful buildings sandwiched together in Mont-Tremblant were strung with golden Christmas lights that also ran over the street. Bells jingled, a Santa ho-ho-ho-ed and posed for photos with bouncy children, and a caroling group sang "God Rest Ye Merry Gentlemen," dressed in matching red hats and gloves.

The temperature was just below freezing and the wind calm, so it was perfect weather to stroll along and watch the holiday bustle under a cloudy sky. Daniel kept close to Cole just in case he felt dizzy suddenly.

*No other reason. Nope.*

He pointed at a patch of ice on the sidewalk. "Watch out for that."

Cole stepped carefully around it. "Thanks. You know, I probably shouldn't remind you, but I'm shocked you're not glued to your phone."

Daniel stopped. "Huh. I didn't even think about it." He realized he hadn't the day before either when he'd come for groceries. The only thing on his mind had been getting back to Cole and making him dinner.

Pulling out his phone, he checked the network. "Yeah, I have three dots." He hesitated, staring at the screen, which was crowded with notifications. Then he turned it off and resolutely put it back in his pocket.

Cole whistled softly. "Look at you CYCing."

They started walking again, and Daniel said, "Sergeant Becky would be proud."

"Sergeant Becky? Seriously? You have got to tell me all about that sometime." He pointed. "Hey, there's a little movie theater. And look what's playing."

Daniel's heart leapt as he spotted the poster in the window of the old-fashioned little cinema. "But you already saw the new *Star Wars* movie."

"I'll totally see it again! If I doze off, no harm,

no foul. Come on, let's check the times."

"You sure you don't mind?"

Cole tugged on Daniel's sleeve. "I'm sure." He scanned the sign. "It's on in French right now, but English is in forty-five minutes. Perfect. Let's go to that chocolate store. We'll have popcorn and candy for lunch because you know what? We can."

Half an hour later, Daniel juggled two large tubs of popcorn—butter layered in the middle as well as on top—and his cola. Cole held his own pop, with the bag from the chocolate shop hooked over his good arm.

Cole asked, "Where do you like to sit?" They were the first ones in the theater, which only had eight rows, but a nice-sized screen.

"The back? I hate people kicking my seat."

"Oh my God, *same.*"

"And there are always too many people in the middle. People are so annoying."

"I'd high five you right now if either of us had a spare hand."

By the time the lights dimmed for the previews, the theater was only half full, most tourists in town likely still on the slopes. A *thwack* made Daniel jump, and Cole whispered, "Sorry. Terry's Chocolate Orange?"

He unwrapped the foil and passed Daniel a segment. Their fingers met, and Daniel's breath stuttered before he reined in the wayward burst of *want.* He shoved the chocolate into his mouth.

*I really am having a nervous breakdown.*

Yet despite his confusion, peace filled him. As the John Williams theme played and the iconic yellow text crawled up the screen, bringing them up to speed on the galactic goings-on, he grinned to himself, happier than he could remember being since the early days with Trevor before it all went to hell.

That life felt a blessedly long time ago and far, far away. Daniel was here with Cole now, and he didn't want to be anywhere else.

"THAT BITCH HAS got to be hot enough by now," Cole said. "It's been more than twenty-four hours."

"A hundred degrees. Perfect, according to the guidelines." Daniel straightened from his crouch by the control panel on the side of the tub. "We can change into our suits and—shit. I didn't bring mine." He slapped his forehead. "I'm such a moron. Who rents a house with a hot tub and doesn't bring their trunks?"

"Oh. It never crossed my mind. I didn't really know where you were bringing me, in my defense. And I was recently concussed." Cole stood by the sliding door into the house. They hadn't opened the glass doors around the hot tub yet. "I mean… We can just go naked, right?" Cole's cheeks went rosy as though he'd gone back out in the cold. "It's only the two of us. But if it's too weird…"

"No, it's fine. Of course." *Yep, it's fine! Not a problem at all! We'll just get naked. No big.* Pulse racing, Daniel scoffed. "We probably saw each other naked a bunch back in the day."

Cole smiled faintly. "A few times, I think."

"We need to cover your cast too. Just in case. There are a couple of bathrobes and slippers in the closet in our room that Justin fortunately didn't find." Daniel led the way, pausing to make sure Cole was okay on the stairs.

*Everything is fine. Nothing to see here. I am not going to lose it.*

He laid the robes on the bed and stripped down, keeping his gaze firmly on the floor. Belting the soft terrycloth robe around him, Daniel turned to find Cole still in his jeans.

"I was just thinking we should cover my cast before I put on the robe." Cole's cheeks were still awfully red.

"Good plan." When Daniel had Cole's arm encased in the plastic glove to his shoulder, he eased up an elastic band to hold it in place. "And just think, you could examine a cow after."

Cole's laughter puffed across Daniel's face. "I'll pass."

"Should I get your jeans?"

Adam's apple bobbing, Cole nodded. "Thanks."

Daniel was only going to pop the button for him since he seemed able to manage the rest, but found himself on his knees, peeling down Cole's jeans and helping him step out of them. He gazed up to find Cole's chest rising and falling rapidly.

*Don't look at his dick. Even though it's right there, do not look.*

Pushing to his feet, Daniel busied himself while Cole worked down his boxer-briefs and wrapped the robe around his shoulders. Cole asked, "Ready?"

Not at all sure of the answer, Daniel nodded regardless.

In the kitchen, he grabbed two plastic wine glasses from a cupboard marked: *For hot tub use.* In his, he poured merlot; in Cole's, OJ. He tucked both bottles under his arm in case they wanted refills.

Cole waited by the sliding glass door. "Thanks. Sorry, I would have taken off the cover, but I don't know if I can drag it with only one hand."

"It's cool. It's surprisingly heavy. You can get the door though."

Cole pulled it back with a flourish, and soon Daniel had stowed the cover, set their drinks in the cup holders, and slid away the far wall, giving them an unimpeded view of the white-capped mountain peaks beyond. The sinking sun glittered like diamonds on the snow of the lake, unbroken but for the odd snowshoe tracks. The wind remained calm.

"Okay." Cole eyed the tub. "Let me just…" He kicked off his slippers. "Cold, cold!" After whipping his robe off his shoulders and onto a wall hook, he went to the hot tub and threw a leg over it.

Naked. Totally naked.

Daniel really tried not to peek at Cole's long, uncut dick hanging from a trimmed thatch of dark hair, his balls low.

He really, *really* tried.

Cole held out his good hand to Daniel. "Um, can you…"

Spurred into action, Daniel took his hand, keeping him steady as he climbed onto the nearest seat, then down into the center of the hot tub.

They were holding hands, and it was warm and slightly sweaty. Daniel almost didn't let go when Cole reached the corner seat on the right side of the tub, where he could sit and rest his left arm along the back.

But he did release Cole's hand, and his voice was almost normal as he asked, "Okay?"

"Yep. Think I'm settled."

Daniel hung up his own robe, kicked off his

slippers, and climbed into the seat in the left corner, sinking under the hot water with an involuntary sigh.

Cole grinned. "Feels great, huh?"

"It does."

"The view is amazing too."

Daniel watched Cole. "It is."

As night fell, the Christmas lights around the porch automatically came on, the tree glowing from inside too. There was something absolutely perfect about being in steamy water while the air was frosty and crisp.

Plus, now that Cole was covered in bubbling water to his chest, his pinkish nipples barely showing in the rhythm of the current, Daniel could relax and stop having inappropriate thoughts.

In three, two, one…

What was the matter with him? He gulped his wine, the dry, fruity aftertaste tingling on his tongue. He had to stop thinking about the way Cole's thighs had flexed when he'd climbed in. How warm and strong his grasp had been holding onto Daniel. How gorgeous his cock was, and how Daniel wanted to suck him and find out what kind of sounds he made when he came.

*Fuck. Me.*

He had to think about *anything* else, because he was getting hard beneath the frothing water. It didn't make any sense. First off, he was supposed to be taking care of Cole, not perving on him. They were sort-of brothers, but no, not really at all.

Still, Cole was younger. And injured. It was wrong. Daniel was supposed to be responsible and trustworthy. When he made director, Martin had told him one of the reasons was because he was so coolheaded. Even-keeled.

So why was he capsized and flailing around?

Also it had only been *days* since he'd met Cole again. He shouldn't be feeling this attraction at all, but certainly not so quickly. This was completely new territory.

He drained his glass, then reached over the side to where he'd left the bottle and refilled it. His skin felt itchy and too-small to contain him. Somehow he'd been scraped raw and vulnerable, this new desire for Cole exposing him and shattering his usual containment.

He ran through a list of hot actors he enjoyed looking at. Yet even if Chris Evans, Chris Hemsworth, *and* Chris Pratt had all magically appeared naked in the hot tub with them, Daniel would only have eyes for Cole.

"You okay?"

Blinking, Daniel forced a smile. "Uh-huh!"

"You looked kind of panicky. Are you getting overheated?"

*Yep, but not in the way you mean.* "I was just thinking about work. All the stuff I'll have to do in January."

Cole gave him a stern look. "No work. My thesis isn't going to write itself, but we are on vacation. Let's worry about all that shit when the time comes. It'll still be there. I promise."

Daniel had to laugh. "You're right. It will."

"But we should make sure we don't get too hot. With the cold air, I think it can be misleading."

He nodded and sipped his wine. Or guzzled it, whichever. After the second glass, he was still half-hard. Cole shifted, and his foot brushed against Daniel's, shooting sparks straight to his balls. Breathing in quiet little pants, Daniel watched Cole sip his orange juice, then lick his lips.

Cole's mouth was on the narrow side, and it glistened after the flick of red tongue. What would it be like to kiss him? To slide his tongue inside? What kind of sounds would Cole make? Would he moan and whimper?

Fuck, Daniel was going to come without even touching himself.

Then somehow he opened his big, dumb mouth and said, "I really want to kiss you."

Eyes wide, Cole stared at him, his glass of OJ halfway to his mouth. "Uh… Huh?"

*Fuck, fuck, shit, piss, fuuuuck.* "Oh my God.

I'm so sorry. I don't know what's wrong with me. I…" He scrambled for some kind of explanation. Two glasses of wine were hardly enough to make him tipsy, let alone drunk. "It must be the heat after all."

"Wait. You want to kiss me? That's what you said. Right? I'm not hearing things?"

Daniel wanted to sink beneath the steaming water and hide, but he answered, "Yes. Cole, I know this is…" *What? What is this?*

"I'm in." Cole nodded emphatically.

"You…really?" A couple of feet separated them in the hot tub, and they stared at each other. Daniel's dick swelled, fire in his veins. Shock, lust, and a flare of joy bubbled together.

Cole slid over and straddled him, leaning his cast on the side of the hot tub beside Daniel's head. Steam rising all around, they groaned as their cocks met. Daniel was thrilled to discover Cole was hard too.

He flattened his hands over Cole's back, touching the flexing muscles there. Cole's tight little body was deliciously heavy, his knees snug around Daniel's hips.

"Holy shit. Is this weird?" Daniel asked, his mind spinning with too many thoughts to capture.

Cole shook his head. "I'm been dreaming of this since I was thirteen."

"Okay, *now* it's weird." He tried to focus on

the man in his lap and not imagine that jug-eared little kid.

Cole laughed. "Shut up." Lips parted, his gaze flicked down to Daniel's mouth and back up again. A drop of water slipped down Cole's forehead, and Daniel raised a hand to brush it away before it could fall into Cole's eyes.

"Daniel, can I kiss you now?"

He could only nod, sucking in a shaky breath as Cole leaned down and met his mouth. It was soft at first, a tentative exploration, their lips parting with little tender kisses. One hand on Cole's waist, Daniel slid the other into Cole's hair, cupping his head and threading his fingers into the short, steam-damp strands. The hot tub hummed, heat enveloping them.

He was *kissing* Cole.

Their noses bumped, and they laughed. A rush of giddiness swirled through Daniel like the bubbling water. It had been since Trevor that he'd kissed anyone, and now he was grateful Justin had been more interested in blowing him to achieve his conquest. Daniel had forgotten just how wonderful it was to taste and tease and share breath. Affection swelled in him.

They deepened the kiss, tongues meeting, stubble rasping. Cole tasted like orange and a hint of chocolate, and Daniel chased the sweetness, running both his hands up and down Cole's back, dipping lower to his ass.

Cole rocked his hips, gasping as he lifted his head, his eyes searching Daniel's. "I love that you're hard for me."

Holding Cole's ass, Daniel arched up, groaning. "I was afraid I would come just thinking about kissing you."

Cole dived for his mouth, thrusting his tongue inside, licking and sucking like he wanted to swallow Daniel whole. They jerked against each other, cocks rubbing in the water. Panting, Cole reached back with his right hand as he leaned heavily against Daniel.

He muttered, "Grab my ass. Spread it."

Daniel was only too happy to follow instructions, but... "We need a condom."

Cole licked across Daniel's mouth. "Not for this. Trust me." He lifted up on his knees and reached back to position Daniel's cock between his cheeks, then squeezed as he lowered down.

The friction was incredible. Daniel moaned, keeping hold of Cole's ass and thrusting up into the narrow cleft. Cole leaned closer, pressing their chests completely together and hooking his chin over Daniel's shoulder. His cock was stiff between them, and it rubbed against Daniel's stomach as they strained together.

Daniel was on fire and *alive*, his unraveling complete. He gripped Cole's ass as Cole writhed against him. Sparks ignited from Daniel's nipples and dick, from every inch of him that Cole touched.

"Fuck," Cole muttered. "I want your cock inside me so bad. But I can't wait. Need to come."

Daniel could only groan, his balls tight. The heat of the water, Cole's body, and the squeeze of his ass cheeks was too much. Daniel's orgasm tore through him, and he thumped his head back as he emptied in spasms, Cole rubbing against him in a frenzy.

The pleasure filled every pore, so much more intense than it was when Daniel jerked off. He trembled.

"That's it," Cole moaned. "Oh fuck, I'm so close. I want you so much."

Pushing one hand between them, Daniel took hold of Cole's cock in the water, stroking and pulling back the foreskin, swirling his thumb over the head. Cole cried out, shaking, and Daniel was pretty sure he was coming.

He squeezed Cole's ass with his left hand, encouraging him to ride it out, jerking him until Cole slumped in his arms, his face against Daniel's neck, mouth open and teeth grazing skin.

Their chests heaved, and Cole lifted his head, pupils blown as if he'd gotten high off some leftover pot. The sun had set, but the Christmas lights shone beyond him. Steam rose in the cold air.

They stared at each other, panting. The hot tub shut off, the cycle finished. Their breath thundered in the sudden quiet.

Had they just made a massive mistake?

Cole grinned. "Guess we have to change the water again before we go."

Relief whooshed through him. Daniel could only hold Cole close and kiss him tenderly as the moon rose over the snowy mountains, joy making itself at home in his heart after so many years gone.

# Chapter Eight

"Tampons, Tums, sunscreen, baby shampoo…" Crouching in his fluffy white robe, Daniel rooted around in the cabinet under one of the sinks in the master bedroom. It was full of random supplies presumably left by other guests.

"How did you not bring condoms and lube on a romantic getaway?" Cole fidgeted and tried not to pace. If they had to go back to the village to stock up, so be it. Because he was getting fucked by Daniel as soon as humanly possible.

Daniel's voice was muffled as he leaned farther into the cabinet. "Justin said he'd take care of it since I was working late all last week."

"I think it was a Freudian thing. Deep down, you knew there was no way you were fucking that asshole. Literally."

Laughing, Daniel leaned back. "Touché. And

ah-ha!" He held up a box of condoms. "Victory."

Desire simmered through Cole, tugging at his groin. *I'm getting Daniel Diaz's cock. I must be freaking dreaming.* "Check the expiry."

Daniel scanned the box. "We're good."

And they *were*. They'd gotten off in the hot tub, and then laughed and kissed. Daniel had made grilled-cheese sandwiches, which they'd eaten in their bathrobes, leaning against the island in the kitchen. It all felt so natural.

They were *good*.

"Let me see if there's any... Holy shit. This place really does have everything." He held up the lube, then touched Cole's right hand. "Cole?"

"Huh? Yeah, that'll work."

Daniel's forehead furrowed. "Are you feeling okay? You seemed kind of spacey there."

"No, I'm great." Cole brushed back a curl from Daniel's forehead. "Just thinking about how crazy this is. How right this feels. You and me."

But now Daniel's frown deepened. Shit, maybe Cole had said too much. *Stupid!* He was going to scare him off. It's not as if they were a *couple* after screwing around in a hot tub.

Daniel stood, leaning beside him against the vanity. He ran a fingertip over the shell of Cole's ear, sending a shiver down his spine, Cole's heart thudding. "But what you said, about wanting it since you were a kid... Is that true? Like, you had a crush on me or something?"

"A massive crush. I told you the other day that you helped me realize I was gay. That wasn't just because of the example you set by coming out. It was because thinking about you gave me a twenty-four-seven boner."

Still holding the box of condoms, Daniel laughed. "You have a way with words."

Cole exhaled. Maybe he hadn't freaked Daniel out too badly after all. "And I'm not a kid now. Obviously."

Daniel gave him a sly look. "Yeah, I noticed." He tugged at the belt on Cole's robe, then sank to his knees in front of him. He looked up under his thick eyelashes. "Can I…?"

"Oh hell yes. Suck me."

"You're kind of bossy." He grinned. "I like it."

Before Cole could respond, Daniel leaned in and nuzzled around the base of his cock, sliding his hands around to take hold of Cole's hips under the open robe. Leaning back against the vanity, Cole gripped the edge of the counter with his good hand.

Gazing up with his beautiful hazel eyes, Daniel licked a stripe from the base of the shaft to the tip. Cole could only moan, his dick pulsing with need.

Daniel was tentative at first, kissing and tasting, sucking on the head and gazing up at him. Cole had the feeling he wanted approval, so he smiled and murmured, "That feels amazing. You're so good at this."

From what Daniel had told him the night before, it had probably been years since he'd last done this, and while he was a little clumsy, it was already the greatest blow job in Cole's life because it was *Daniel* on his knees for him.

Daniel's pretty eyelashes fanned over his golden-brown cheeks as he sucked harder, taking him in deeper, his hand circling the base of Cole's dick, tongue exploring and teasing the foreskin. His breath catching, goosebumps broke over Cole in waves.

He wished desperately he had two usable hands. He let go of the counter, hoping Daniel's grasp on his hips would be enough to keep him on his feet as his knees shook.

Threading his fingers into Daniel's curls, Cole cradled his head and asked, "Are you hard?"

Looking up, his full lips stretched around Cole's cock, Daniel sucked hard before he pulled off with a wet smack that echoed deliciously off the tile. Sitting back on his heels, he tugged open his robe to show his thick, meaty cock curving up, straining and flushed red. The glistening head peeked out from his foreskin.

"Fuck, you're beautiful. That's so good." Cole caressed Daniel's head. "I can't wait to get that inside me." Heart galloping, he asked, "Do you like rimming? When I first saw it in porn, I thought about you doing it to me. I—" He sucked in a breath as Daniel spun him around, grabbing for the counter with his good hand and ignoring the flare of pain in his left.

Daniel hauled up Cole's robe and spread his ass, and Cole bent over the counter, parting his legs wider. He panted, "I'll take that as a *yessss*."

He groaned as Daniel licked up and down his crease, toying with his hole before pushing into it. The counter dug into Cole's belly, and his head thumped against the mirror, but he moaned, "Don't stop. More."

Hot exhalations washed over Cole's tender flesh. Daniel leaned back a few inches and spit before burying his face between Cole's cheeks, licking into him and eating his ass. Legs jerking, Cole's breath steamed up the mirror. His dick leaked, and he cried out, never wanting it to end, but also desperate for more.

"Fuck me. Please. I need your cock."

Cole moaned when Daniel gave him a parting kiss on his hole, watching in the mirror as he stood behind him. Their gazes locked, and Daniel said, "On the bed."

Cole was happy to get fucked anywhere Daniel wanted to do it. Nodding, he followed into the bedroom, tugging off his robe, swearing when the sleeve got caught on his cast before he could toss it aside.

"Careful." Naked now too, Daniel caught Cole around his waist, bending to brush their lips together. He whispered, "I don't want to hurt you."

Cole's heart glowed as brightly as the Christmas lights. "You won't." He backed up and turned to knee-walk onto the bed before flattening out on his back. "Can you put a pillow under my cast?" He stretched his arm out so his hand would be well free of their bodies.

Daniel did as he asked, then kneeled by Cole's feet, waiting and seemingly uncertain. He'd brought the condoms and lube, and Cole said, "Get yourself ready. Stop worrying." He rubbed his foot over Daniel's thigh. "I promise I'll tell you if anything hurts. Okay?"

"Okay." Daniel gave him a little smile that made Cole's heart clench.

After rolling on the condom, Daniel slicked himself, biting his reddened lip with a little moan. Cole spread his legs and lifted his knees, offering himself. Fuck, he *loved* cock, and knowing that he was actually going to have Daniel's made his head spin. He groaned, his dick jumping as Daniel pushed a slick finger into him.

"Uh-huh, I'm ready. I'm *so* ready." Cole grasped at Daniel's shoulder with his right hand, tugging him closer. "Fuck me." He shoved his tongue in Daniel's mouth, tasting the musky hint of himself.

When Daniel inched into him, gritting his teeth, his nostrils flaring, Cole bore down, urging him deeper, loving the burn as Daniel stretched him open.

"Fuck, Cole." Daniel's arms quivered where he held himself up.

"I know." He lifted his tailbone and hooked his legs around Daniel's waist. "Harder. I need it. I know you won't hurt me. Orgasm is the best medicine for a fading concussion and broken bones."

The burst of Daniel's laughter puffed across Cole's face. They kissed messily as Daniel rocked into him, settling into a rhythm, filling Cole completely.

"Never thought I'd have this again," Daniel mumbled. He gasped as Cole tightened his inner muscles around him, snapping his hips and really *pounding* him now.

Cole could have died happy, being plowed by Daniel Diaz. The real thing was so much better than even his most detailed fantasy. He couldn't have truly imagined the salty taste of Daniel's sweat on his tongue, the way he whimpered, red lips parted, staring into Cole's eyes as if nothing else in the world existed.

And it didn't. It was only the two of them,

gasping and kissing and fucking.

When Cole came, he painted his chest without his dick even being touched. Daniel pressed against the perfect spot inside him, and Cole spurted until he could only quiver and moan, his balls emptying.

He squeezed around Daniel's cock. "I want you inside me forever."

"Oh!" Daniel whipped his head back, spine arching as he came. He collapsed onto Cole, panting against his cheek in warm gusts, their skin sticky and slick.

Cole kept his legs wrapped tightly around Daniel. Maybe it was crazy, but forever sounded about right.

# Chapter Nine

"ARE YOU SURE you don't want to go skiing? I don't want to hold you back." Cuddled on the couch, Cole trailed his fingers up and down Daniel's arm. Christmas Eve had dawned cloudy with snow in the forecast, and Cole would be content to stay exactly where he was, but guilt that Daniel was missing out nagged.

They'd spent two days fucking every which way they could imagine with the limitations of Cole's cast. His ass was pleasantly sore, and his jaw ached from sucking off Daniel for ages that morning, edging him and not letting him come until Daniel had begged so prettily.

"I've actually never gone skiing before. I'd probably end up in a cast to match yours."

Cole laughed. "They must have a lot of other activities."

"Hmm. Maybe there's something we can do

together." Daniel shifted Cole's feet off his lap and stood to reach for a brochure sitting on the coffee table. He sat back down, and even though Cole had bent his legs, Daniel took his feet and pulled them across his lap again, warm and secure.

He opened the brochure. "Let's see. Alpine touring—looks like we'd be hiking with ski poles, so that's out. Biking, cross-country skiing, downhill skiing, dogsledding, ice climbing—hell no—tubing, skating…" He flipped the pages. "I don't think any of these are broken-limb friendly. Oh wait! We could go on a sleigh ride."

"Tempting as that is, I think I'll pass. Maybe we should just head into the village and restock on food? Get some milk and cookies for Santa tonight. Ohhh, and eggnog."

"Eggnog?" Daniel scrunched up his face.

"Have you actually tried it?"

"Well…no. Not since I was a kid."

"A-ha! I'll get the stuff for my mom's secret recipe. You'll be converted, I swear." He thought of her with a familiar pang of grief, sharp, then dull again before fading into the background and never quite going away.

"Okay. I'll try it."

"Speaking of moms, what do you think Claudia's going to say? About us? I think she'll be good. Right?"

"Well, she already loves you, so yeah. I think

she'll be jazzed. Once she gets over any weirdness. What about your dad?"

Cole pondered it. "He probably barely remembers you at this point, so I can't see why he'd care."

Daniel laughed. "True enough." He tossed the brochure back on the table and slid his hand along Cole's shin under his PJs. "I really don't mind just chilling instead of hitting the slopes. I haven't relaxed like this in…" His brow furrowed.

"No, don't frown! Stop thinking about it. You frown too much."

"I do?" Naturally, Daniel frowned.

"Yeah. I mean, you can do whatever you want to do. You just seem like you're anxious a lot. Stressed."

Daniel toyed with the hair on Cole's leg. He smiled softly. "I guess I am." Then he blinked and jerked his head, as if taken aback. "I haven't thought about work at *all* today! Huh. That's so weird."

"Well, don't start now." Cole sat up and drew him close for a kiss, rubbing his thumb over the stubble on Daniel's cheek. "Let's resupply, then we can hibernate until it's time to go home."

He wasn't sure what would happen to the happy little bubble they'd constructed when they went back to real life in Ottawa, but Cole chased the worry away. They'd take each day as it came.

SHIVERING, COLE JAMMED his right fist deeper into his pockets. "The wind chill has got to be minus thirty." His nose hair was stiff, little frozen icicles lining his nostrils. His fingertips tingled where they peeked out from his cast.

Daniel stopped short as they hurried from the parking lot toward the main area of the village. "Don't you have gloves?"

Cole held up his cast. "This presents a challenge."

"But your other hand!" Daniel stripped off his right glove and passed it over.

"Now you'll be cold!"

"I'll put my hand in my pocket. Come on. This way we'll each have one warm hand, at least."

Cole tried not to smile too much. "Okay. Thanks."

After stocking up on some alcohol and what was likely way too much food, they stowed the groceries in the car and headed back to the main street to grab takeout. Cole squinted at the red sign toward the end of the pedestrian street. "Is that a BeaverTails down there? I could really go for some warm sugary goodness."

"I'm not sweet enough?" Daniel gave him a cheesy wink.

"As sweet as you are, there's something irresistible about fried dough."

Daniel grinned. "You want to pick some up while I hit Coco Pazzo for our lunch?" He nodded to the nearby restaurant. "It says on the awning they do takeout. Unless you want to sit down and eat?"

"Nah. There will be other people there. At the chalet, it's just you and me. And the hot tub." He waggled his eyebrows and lifted his gloved hand for a high five.

With a laugh, Daniel slapped his palm. "Sounds like a plan. You have any allergies or stuff you don't like? Maybe you should come look at the menu. It'll probably take a while for them to make the food, so you'll have time to go after. Oh, we should get more challah from that bakery."

"I'll grab it on my way. And I'm easy. Get whatever you want for lunch. How about you? Anything you don't like? And there might be nuts in the pastries." He didn't remember Daniel having allergies, but people could develop them.

"I'm easy too."

"I know, but do you have any allergies?"

Daniel's laughter followed Cole on the wind as Cole hurried down the street. The golden Christmas lights strung across the pedestrian street and around poles shone merrily in the cloudy dullness. Salt crunched underfoot, and giant green and red wreathes decorated the streetlights. People bustled around, excited chatter and children's voices ringing in the air.

A little girl in a puffy blue snowsuit squealed in front of a store window displaying a massive dollhouse with various holiday scenes acted out inside by toy humans, mice, and what looked to be beavers. She pointed and laughed, her parents grinning.

Cole paused to take in the display too, and was about to hurry on when he spotted something inside the store beyond the dollhouse. Heart skipping, he pushed open the door, sighing in relief at the blast of warm air.

The shop carried home furnishings and knick-knacks, and had a large selection of holiday decorations. Cole peered up at the top of a Christmas tree, excitement zipping through him. It was absolutely perfect. He didn't care how much it cost—Daniel had to have it.

A saleswoman approached, and Cole pointed to the tree topper and said, "Sold."

After buying the pastries and bread, he tucked the tree topper box in the bottom of the bakery bag. He tried to wipe the smile off his face as he rejoined Daniel inside Coco Pazzo's small takeout area, which was wonderfully warm and smelled of tomatoes and garlic and everything delicious.

"What?" Daniel asked.

"Huh? Nothing. I'm just happy."

Daniel frowned, but Cole could tell he was putting it on. "Are you sure you're not concussed again? What's your name?"

"Cole Smith, and I'm having the best Christmas ever. Maybe except for the one year my mom took me to Disney World." He pretended to ponder it. "Nope. Sorry, Mickey. This is the best."

Daniel's cheeks creased. "Me too. I still can't get over how surreal this is. In a good way."

"It really is." Cole's nose was thawing in the warmth, his cheeks tingling. His stomach rumbled, and he took off his glove and managed to open the BeaverTails box, tearing off the corner of one of the long, flat pastries that were shaped in rounded rectangles.

He held out the dough for Daniel. "I figured we can share. I got maple, classic cinnamon and sugar, and this one. Nutella."

With a low groan, Daniel took the sweet, sticky goodness, licking his lips. Cole had a piece too, and as he licked his fingers, Daniel watched with hooded eyes, leaning closer.

A woman cleared her throat. "Charcuterie platter, calamari, trotta affumicatta, gnocchi with gorgonzola, two lamb shanks, and the spaghettini con anatra."

Boggling, Cole asked Daniel, "Did you invite Justin and the gang back?"

"I figured leftovers wouldn't go astray. And I

wasn't sure what you liked."

"So he got everything," the woman agreed cheerfully. "You boys have a merry Christmas."

Cole managed to wait until they were back in the car before launching himself at Daniel for hazelnut-chocolate kisses.

COLE NUZZLED THE back of Daniel's neck, his breath ticklish, stubble rough. "Merry Christmas," Cole whispered, pressed up behind him. He had put on his flannel PJ bottoms, and they rubbed softly against the curve of Daniel's ass.

"Mmm."

"Did I wear you out last night, sleepyhead?"

A bolt of pleasure shot down Daniel's spine at the memory of Cole riding him, his thighs flexing and cock bobbing, managing better than they'd expected, leaning his good hand against Daniel's chest and leaving imprints of his fingernails. Daniel couldn't remember ever having so much *fun* during sex as he did with Cole.

He opened his eyes, blinking at the dull light that shone in, clouds filling the slice of sky he could see through the parted curtains. "Is it snowing?"

"It is. Santa had his work cut out for him last night. Perfect day to stay inside by a roaring fire.

But apparently fire building is a two-hand job, so time to get up."

Turning his head, Daniel gave him a kiss. "You really are bossy. I still like it."

Naked, Daniel shuffled into the bathroom to piss and wash his face before pulling on his silk PJ bottoms and a sweatshirt. Cole had gone back downstairs, and the aroma of brewing coffee wafted up.

On the stairs, Daniel breathed it in deeply, admiring the view of the fresh snow through the wide windows and the Christmas tree that—

He stumbled on the last step, catching himself, then walking slowly on bare feet toward the tree, which was lit up in all its glittering glory. The star that had sat atop it was gone. Daniel blinked up at the replacement.

It was *Yoda.*

With a *glowing green lightsaber.* Green-skinned Yoda wore a sandy-brown robe with a white robe over top. His wrinkled face was wonderfully detailed, and he held up the lightsaber on a diagonal.

"Merry Christmas, and may the force be with us."

Daniel spun around to find Cole biting his lip, clearly trying not to grin, scratching at his bare chest. Daniel looked back at the tree, then Cole. "How? When? Where?"

"I spotted it yesterday when I went to Beaver-Tails. I thought a Yoda tree topper was something you needed in your life."

"I do. I absolutely do." He'd needed so many things in his life and hadn't realized *how* much. "Thank you." He pulled Cole into a hug, leaning down to kiss his cheek.

Cole's body fit perfectly in Daniel's arms. It had been too long since he'd been able to just hug someone for longer than a greeting with his mom or Pam. He inhaled deeply, smelling soap, a hint of pine, and *Cole.*

"I'm melting," he murmured.

Cole leaned back. "Is it too hot in here? Do you not want to start a fire?"

"No, I mean…" Daniel ran his thumb over Cole's bottom lip. "I was frozen inside, and now I'm melting all over the place. This is crazy, right? The other shoe is going to drop any second."

"Nope." Cole inched closer, stepping lightly on Daniel's feet with his icy feet. "No shoes here." He wriggled his toes and slid his good arm around Daniel's waist. "Although I think the fire is a good idea. Right after you kiss me again."

With a smile, Daniel followed instructions, and soon he had the kindling sparked, rolled newspaper flaming and catching the log. Cole brought him coffee, and they sat cross-legged on the fake fur rug in front of the hearth by the

Christmas tree, sipping from their mugs.

"You know what we should do today?" Cole asked.

Daniel swallowed his mouthful of rich, bitter coffee. "What?"

"This. Plus the hot tub and maybe a couple movies. Italian food leftovers. Oh, and fucking." Cole nodded seriously. "Definitely more fucking." He knee-walked to the tree and reached beneath it, pulling out the bottle of lube.

Daniel didn't know the last time he'd laughed so much as he had the past few days. His shoulders shook, and he pressed his hands around his still-warm mug. "What about a condom?"

Reaching up, Cole plucked a foil wrapper from the tree. "There are a few more hidden in there. Santa believes in safe sex." He caught the edge of the wrapper between his teeth, picked up the lube, and shuffled back to Daniel.

Daniel took the condom, his stomach swooping like he was riding a rollercoaster at Canada's Wonderland. "What do you think about fucking me this time?"

Cole's breath shuddered, his lips parting. "Yeah? You're up for that?"

"You're the one who'll have to get it up." He laughed at his own stupid joke.

Cole grinned. "Oh, I assure you that won't be an issue."

"What about your hand? How should we…"

"Hmm." He glared at his cast, then scooted closer, running his palm over Daniel's thigh, fingers soft on the silk. "How do you like it?"

Daniel knew he was blushing, his skin going hot down his sternum. "However we can make it work." It had been since Trevor, and the idea of having Cole inside him had his heart drumming.

"But if you had to choose?" Cole stroked Daniel's leg and licked his lips, watching him intently. Cole was so confident with sex, and it made Daniel's dick swell.

"On my hands and knees," he murmured. "You behind me."

"Uh-huh." Cole nodded, capturing Daniel's lips in a hard kiss. "That sounds A-plus."

He sucked in a breath. "But your hand?"

"I can balance. Let's do this." Cole slid his hand over Daniel's growing cock, rubbing him through the silk. "You want to come on my dick?"

Nodding, Daniel pulled him close for another kiss, pushing his tongue into Cole's mouth. Heat radiated through him, his head spinning with lust—with the need to get closer.

"Get naked," Cole commanded, and Daniel scrambled to obey. Still in his pajama bottoms, Cole sat back on his heels, his Adam's apple bobbing as his gaze skated over Daniel's body.

Goosebumps rippled across Daniel's naked

flesh, and he waited on his knees, facing Cole.

"When I have full use of both hands, I'm going to rim you and finger fuck you until you're begging for me. But for now, get yourself ready." He nodded to the lube.

Blood rushing in his ears, Daniel squeezed the cool gel onto his fingers. The fluffy rug was soft under his knees as he reached behind to push a finger into his ass. The fire flickered to his left, Cole in front of him, the Christmas tree's colored lights glowing over Cole's skin.

Daniel couldn't stop the groan that slipped out as he impatiently shoved his finger inside, his hole burning as it stretched. "Fuck," he muttered.

With his good hand, Cole squeezed himself through his PJs. "Feel good?"

"It will." He grunted, squeezing in another slick finger.

"Don't hurt yourself." Cole's brow furrowed.

"Uh-huh." Dropping onto his left hand, Daniel twisted his wrist, pushing past the burn. He kept his head up, meeting Cole's avid gaze.

"Fuck, I wish we had a dildo. Look at you. You're so hot. And you want *my* cock." Cole shook his head like he couldn't believe it. His chest rose and fell quickly, his nipples peaked and flushed red.

Moaning, Daniel pulled out his hand and spread his discarded sweatshirt on the rug. He crawled over and grabbed the condom. Cole sat up on his knees and let Daniel tug his PJs down around his thighs, freeing his leaking cock.

In a warm gust, Cole exhaled sharply as Daniel rolled the condom onto him. His right hand landed on Daniel's shoulder, fingers digging in. Daniel slicked a ton of lube over the condom, and they kissed messily with little moans.

Daniel broke the kiss, his throat dry. "Fuck me. I want you so much. Need you."

Cole's pupils were blown dark. "You've got me. Turn around."

On his hands and knees, Daniel gripped his sweatshirt with slick fingers, making sure it was spread under him. He reached back with his left hand, pulling on his ass cheek as Cole did the same with the right.

It took a few tries, but then Cole had the slippery head of his cock nudging at Daniel's hole. Grunting, he held onto Daniel's right shoulder and pushed.

The air punched out of Daniel's lungs, pain sharp in his ass, Cole's cock feeling impossibly huge. Opening his mouth, he sucked in little gasps of air and shoved back, more than willing to take the discomfort to be filled. He hadn't realized how much he'd needed this.

"Oh, fuck. You're so tight." Cole's fingers dug into Daniel's shoulder as he inched inside. "Tell me if it's too much."

"Don't stop." Daniel's arms and legs quivered, sweat dampening the nape of his neck. "I want this. Want you. Trust you."

For a few moments, Cole didn't move, and his hand loosened, stroking Daniel's shoulder. Then his soft lips pressed to the knobs of Daniel's spine.

Daniel whimpered. "Please."

After another tender kiss, Cole gave it to him, finally pushing past the ring of muscle and slamming all the way home, his balls bouncing off Daniel's ass. They both cried out, and Daniel stared at the white fake fur rug.

He was so full he was afraid he'd split apart, but soon enough his body adjusted, and Cole began rocking in and out. Not much at first, then harder and harder until he was fucking Daniel relentlessly, their skin slapping, slick with sweat, the fire blazing beside them.

It blazed in Daniel as well, the stretch better than he remembered it. The sensation of fullness and brushes against his prostate revived his hard-on, and he could only moan and grunt, forming actual words too difficult.

Cole's rhythm stuttered. "Fuck, I'm going to come. It's too good."

"Do it," Daniel growled. He squeezed around Cole, who held his shoulder hard enough to bruise as he thrust a few more times before jerking and moaning.

Gasping, Cole folded over Daniel's back. "Fuck," Cole muttered, lips wet against Daniel's spine.

Since he was on his hands and knees, Daniel couldn't touch himself, and his dick strained. Cole couldn't touch him either, apparently hanging on for dear life with his good hand. Daniel whimpered low in his throat.

Panting, Cole lifted off, awkwardly rolling onto his right side on the rug. "On your back." He urged Daniel to flip over and said, "Feed it to me." He bent over and latched his mouth onto Daniel's cock.

It was so wet and hot and *good*, and Daniel groaned and shoved his hips up, only needing a few thrusts before his balls drew up and he came. The pleasure seared white hot, shuddering through him as he emptied into Cole's mouth.

Cole swallowed as much as he could, and some of Daniel's spunk dripped from the corners of his lips. "Oh fuck," Daniel groaned. He reached up and caught a few drops with his fingers, and Cole licked and sucked them clean too.

Chests heaving, they looked at each other and laughed. Careful of his cast, Cole snuggled close, draping his left arm over Daniel's belly. "Merry Christmas to us."

"God bless us everyone," Daniel agreed.

"It's even better than I imagined." Cole sighed contentedly, kissing Daniel's nipple. "And I imagined it a lot over the years. In so many ways."

In the colorful glow of the Christmas tree, snow fell beyond the huge windows. The fire crackled beside them, and they were quiet. Peaceful. Daniel traced the bumps of Cole's spine. "It shouldn't be this easy."

"Hmm?" His warm breath teased Daniel's chest hair.

"This, I mean. You and me. We just met— well, again. But it's only been days. How can it feel so right? Have I just been alone for too long?"

"Hey!" Cole poked him in the side with his finger.

"I didn't mean it like that." Daniel laughed. "Obviously you're amazing." He kissed the top of Cole's head.

"It's true. If you were just desperate for any-one, you'd still be with that douchecanoe."

Daniel shuddered. "I'm so glad you're a klutz."

"It has never come in more handy." Cole snorted. "Get it?"

They laughed, shaking in each other's arms. Daniel sighed. "It just feels *right* with you. I can't explain it."

"Maybe it's a Christmas miracle. But, you know, my aunt and uncle got together super quick. They had lunch with some mutual friends. I can't remember why. But at one point, Aunt Judy left to use the bathroom, and Uncle Steve said, 'That's the woman I'm going to marry.' And he did. Been together decades and have three kids. They just knew it was right."

Daniel swallowed over the sudden lump in his throat. Even with the warmth of the fire on his skin, a shiver ran over him. "Do you think this is right? Us?"

Cole nuzzled his stubbly face against Daniel's pec. "I think it really could be. I guess we'll find out."

"I guess we will." He stared up at the distant beams of the cathedral ceiling, grinning. A log sparked, and he glanced at the fireplace. Then he jolted, realizing the stockings were now full. "Wait, you bought stocking stuffers too? I didn't get you anything!"

Cole shrugged. "It's all stuff from around the house. Spoiler alert: I know you were eyeing those Tums."

Laughing, Daniel took Cole's face in his hands and drew him up for a kiss. Or two. Or five. Ten, perhaps. Catching his breath, Daniel murmured, "Next year, I'm going to get you everything you could possibly want for Christmas."

Eyes bright, Cole grinned. "Next year, huh?"

When Daniel thought of his future now, yep—there was Cole. "Definitely."

"I'll drink to that. Hey, the doc said I should be good by now to 'indulge,' as she put it. Let me pour eggnog Mom-style while you stoke the fire." Cole carefully sat and pulled up his pajama bottoms.

Smiling to himself and gazing up at Yoda every so often, Daniel pulled on his own PJs and hurried out for more logs, which were stacked under a tarp beyond the hot tub on the porch. The flames leapt again by the time Cole joined him with two small glasses full of thick, off-white nog.

"So, her secret recipe was mixing eggnog with Amaretto. Maybe calling it a 'recipe' was a stretch." He handed over a glass, and they clinked.

Daniel took a sip. "Mmm. I love it!" Actually, it was cloyingly sweet and he didn't really like the texture of cream, which was one of the reasons eggnog had never been his favorite.

Cole's gaze narrowed. "You're so full of shit. But thank you for trying it." He leaned in for a soft kiss.

"Anything for you," Daniel told him, and he knew it was true.

# Epilogue

*A year later*

"COLE, YOU'VE BEEN such a wonderful influence. There's actual *color* in this house!" Claudia exclaimed. "A real Christmas tree!" She fingered the fresh pine needles.

Cole couldn't resist saying, "There's debate about whether real or artificial has more environmental impact, but we decided to support a local business instead of buying something plastic shipped from China."

"And you can't beat that smell." She inhaled deeply. "Your Yoda angel is a hoot."

"Thanks. We like it." The other ornaments were a mix of *Star Wars* and traditional sparkly balls and snowflakes. The colored lights glowed and silver icicles shimmered. Brightly wrapped gifts spilled out under the tree, too many to be contained.

"Oh, and I love the purple rug," Claudia added.

From the office down the hall, Daniel shouted, "I'll have you know I bought that rug before I met Cole! Well, before I met him again."

Cole laughed. "But I'm responsible for the burgundy tea towels in the kitchen." He'd moved in with Daniel that summer, and it felt like they'd been together forever. Life was super weird sometimes, but in the best way.

He asked Claudia, "Are you sure you don't want anything to eat?"

"No, no. The dinner on the train was surprisingly good. I'm so glad I splurged on first class." She winked and ran a hand over her perfectly coiffed brown curls. "I'm worth it."

"You definitely are. You look amazing, by the way."

She practically glowed. "Thank you, sweetheart. I tell you, I owe it all to Pilates. And Pierre."

Claudia's newish boyfriend had already gone up to bed, but Cole lowered his voice anyway. "He's very handsome."

"Isn't he?" She beamed. "I think he might be the one."

"I hope so." He really, really did.

"Are your aunt and uncle settled?"

"Yeah. It was a long day flying from Winnipeg

with the delay connecting through Toronto." Shrieks of laughter echoed up from the basement, and Cole grinned. "I'm sure the kids will be awake way too late playing video games, but they're all set with their sleeping bags."

Cole hadn't expected Aunt Judy and Uncle Steve to take him up on his invite to spend the holidays in Ottawa, but it was awesome to have family around. With Daniel's friend Pam and her girlfriend coming for dinner the next day, they'd have a full house.

"Christmas Eve is meant for staying up late," Claudia said. "The little bastards have so much sugar in them they won't need sleep."

Laughing, Cole took his buzzing phone from his pocket and read the screen. "My dad says hi, and merry Christmas."

She smiled. "Well, tell Bill the same right back. You know, your father's a real piece of work, but if I hadn't made the mistake of marrying him, we wouldn't have you in our lives." She took Cole's chin and kissed his cheek. "I love you. Sleep tight and dream of lots of sugarplums."

"You too."

Once she was upstairs, Cole flicked off the kitchen light and went to drag Daniel away from his desk. As soon as he walked into the little office, Daniel said, "I know, I know. I'm coming."

*Not yet, but you will be.* Cole stood behind

Daniel's chair, teasing his curls and peeking over his shoulder at the paperwork on the desk. "What can't wait until the new year? The office closed today at noon, didn't it?"

"Uh-huh." Daniel's pen scratched over the paper. "I implemented a new staff information form and said they had to be filled out before Christmas. Just living up to my end of the bargain. I'm almost done."

"Hey, have you heard if Justin has found a new job yet?"

Daniel glanced up, trying not to smile. "Not yet. Turns out when you lie about your qualifications and are crappy at your job, it's hard to find a new position."

"Couldn't have happened to a better asshole."

As Daniel chuckled and went back to the form, Cole rubbed Daniel's neck and said, "You're not supposed to work on our anniversary week."

"It's a whole week now, hmm?"

"Yep. It's a new thing."

Daniel grinned. "You know what? You're right—this can wait." He straightened the papers and left them in a neat pile on the side of the desk. "Let's go celebrate. Quietly."

"And unlike last year, I have full use of both my hands. And I know how to use them."

"I am well aware." Daniel pushed back his chair and stood, kissing Cole soundly and holding him close. "I love you."

"Love you too. Maybe next year we can go back to Tremblant. You, me, a hot tub."

"It's a date. We'll alternate. One Christmas with the fam, one Christmas at our private chalet." He tugged Cole around the desk and into the hall. "Oh, wait. I need my charging cable. Want to make sure I can take pictures tomorrow morning."

"I'll grab it. Go on up."

Cole ducked back into the office, flipping on the light. Behind the desk, he unplugged the cable from the laptop port. Then he glanced at the form Daniel had been filling out.

A line caught his eye before he went back upstairs, grinning the whole way, his heart full.

*In case of emergency, contact: Cole Smith; domestic partner; 343-555-555*

## THE END

Thank you so much for reading *In Case of Emergency*! I hope you enjoyed Cole and Daniel's story, and I'd be grateful if you could take a few minutes to leave a review on Amazon, Goodreads, BookBub, or social media. Just a couple of sentences can really help other readers discover the book. Thank you again.

Wishing you many happily ever afters!

Keira
<3

P.S. Keep reading for a sneak peek at another steamy and sweet holiday romance!

## Will friends become lovers this Christmas?

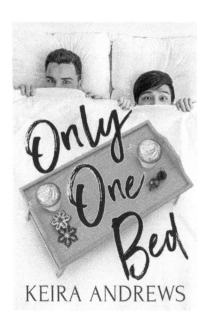

**Will friends become lovers this Christmas?**

**Sam**

People joke that Etienne and I are boyfriends, but whatever.

Sure, I think about him all the time—he's my best friend. If I've missed him way more than I expected when he left to train with a new skating coach, that's because he's so easy to hang with. And yeah, he's gay, but he's not into me. Why would he be? I'm straight.

We're not *boyfriends*.

But now Etienne needs me, so I'm rushing to the mountain village where he's skating in a holiday show. That's what best friends do.

**Etienne**

I know Sam will never like me the way I like him.

Never *love* me the way I love him.

But now that my competitive skating career might be suddenly ending, I need my best friend by my side. Thank god Sam's spending the holidays with me.

It's okay that he'll never love me back.

It's okay that there's only one bed in this cozy little cabin.

We're best friends. Nothing's going to happen.

*Only One Bed* by Keira Andrews is a gay Christmas story featuring friends to lovers, forced proximity, bisexual awakening, first times, snowy holiday vibes, and of course a happy ending.

**Will fake boyfriends become the real deal this holiday?**

It's the most wonderful time of the year—except ex-Marine Logan is jobless and getting evicted. Worse, he's a new single dad with a stepson who hates him. A kid needs stability—not to mention presents under the tree—and Logan's desperate.

Then he meets lonely Seth and makes a deal.

Can Logan temporarily pretend to be live-in boyfriends to increase Seth's chances at a promotion? If it provides a roof over their heads for the holidays, hell yeah. Logan considers himself straight—he doesn't count occasional hookups with guys—but he can fake it. Besides, with his shy little smile, Seth is surprisingly sexy.

Make that *damn* sexy.

Shocked that Seth has only been with one man, Logan can't resist sweetening their deal to teach him the joys of casual sex. No strings attached. No feelings. No kissing. No commitment.

No falling for each other.

Easy, right?

*The Christmas Deal* is a steamy holiday gay romance from Keira Andrews featuring fake boyfriends, bisexual awakening, a clueless single dad with an angry preteen, and of course a happy ending.

**A nice boy gets naughty...**

Redheaded freshman Jeremy "Cherry" Rourke is certainly living up to his childhood nickname, although still being inexperienced is the least of his concerns. After coming out, his parents barely talk to him. He hasn't made any friends at university. Worst of all, he's about to spend Christmas completely alone in an empty dorm.

Jeremy clearly needs a fairy godfather, so football captain Max Pimenta takes him under his wing to help him find his dating groove. But Jeremy's wound way too tight. He's too vulnerable. Max can't trust some random guy with him. He needs to take care of Jeremy himself and introduce him to no-pressure exploration. It's not about romance or feelings—he's just doing the kid a favor.

**Max is definitely not falling for this lonely, beautiful boy. No way.**
And it's not like he can leave Jeremy all alone for the holidays. He'll bring him home to his family's maple syrup farm—strictly as friends since his parents have rules. No more fooling around. No more eager, breathless fun. No more making Jeremy shiver and blush with suggestive whispers in his ear. No more sweeter-than-sugar kisses. All nice. No more naughty.

But Jeremy's sleeping right across the hall, and Max wants him for himself. The twelve days of Christmas will last an eternity if they don't break the rules.

**Shhh. No one has to know…**
*Merry Cherry Christmas* is a feel-good holiday MM romance from Keira Andrews featuring a nervous nerd and protective, jealous jock, forced proximity, first times, and of course a happy ending.

# About the Author

Keira aims for the perfect mix of character, plot, and heat in her M/M romances. She writes everything from swashbuckling pirates to heart-warming holiday escapism. Her fave tropes are enemies to lovers, age gaps, forced proximity, and passionate virgins. Although she loves delicious angst along the way, Keira guarantees happy endings!

**Discover more at:**
**www.keiraandrews.com**